THE DOWNLOADED

PRAISE FOR *THE DOWNLOADED*

"Robert J. Sawyer's new novel is a potent distillation of everything that makes science fiction so addictive. In the space of a concise and tightly plotted story, *The Downloaded* explores a broad swath of future history and absolutely sizzles with fascinating ideas. You want space travel, a ruined Earth, virtual worlds, a cast of relatable characters, and a glimpse into the labyrinth of human destiny? Look no further: this book has all that and more."

—**Robert Charles Wilson**, Hugo Award-winning author of *Spin*

"In *The Downloaded*, Robert J. Sawyer proves he's not just a master of using science fiction to address social issues but also a master of devious plot twists and diverse character voices."

—**James Alan Gardner**, Theodore Sturgeon Award-winning author of *Commitment Hour*

"No one does the end of the world quite like Robert J. Sawyer. *The Downloaded* is a wicked-smart thrill ride from start to finish. The interview format brings genuine intimacy to this action-packed story that also raises questions about consciousness, society, and the very nature of humanity. I loved it."

—**Sylvain Neuvel**, bestselling author of *A History of What Comes Next*

"Robert J. Sawyer is well known for big-concept original SF and rigorous research. While *The Downloaded* continues in this vein, it's also a wonderful demonstration of another aspect of this impressive author: his deep understanding of— and compassion for—people, regardless who or what they are, or even what they have done. It's a rare and potent humanity that elevates Sawyer's work high above the rest."

—**Julie E. Czerneda**, Aurora Award-winning author of *To Each This World*

"One of the best SF novels I've read in years. *The Downloaded* is a tightly-written SF story that will hold your attention, but it's more than just that. Sawyer has given us an advance look at a technology that we may have someday if we're fortunate, but also a near-future world that we may get, too, and God help us if we do. The juxtaposition of the two makes this a fascinating tale."

—**Allen Steele**, Hugo Award-winning author of *Coyote*

"Extraordinarily well done. Sawyer gives just enough science to make the story's logic utterly plausible—and then he instantly moves on, making the story's focus far more on the emotional impact on the characters rather than on world-building. *The Downloaded* stays honed to the human interest throughout."

—Hugo and Sturgeon Award finalist **Paddy Forde**

PRAISE FOR ROBERT J. SAWYER

"A new Robert J. Sawyer book is always cause for celebration."

—Analog Science Fiction and Fact

"Sawyer not only has an irresistibly engaging narrative voice but also a gift for confronting thorny philosophical conundrums. At every opportunity, he forces his readers to think while holding their attention with ingenious premises and superlative craftsmanship."

—Booklist

"Can Sawyer write? Yes—with near-Asimovian clarity, with energy and drive, with such grace that his writing becomes invisible as the story comes to life in your mind."

—Orson Scott Card

"Robert J. Sawyer is by any measure one of the world's leading (and most interesting) science-fiction writers. His fiction is a fascinating blend of intellectually compelling big ideas and humane, enduring characters."

—The Globe and Mail

"Sawyer, an articulate fountain of ideas, is the genre's northern star—in fact, one of the hottest SF writers anywhere. By any reckoning Sawyer is among the most successful Canadian authors ever."

—Maclean's: Canada's National Magazine

"Robert J. Sawyer is a writer of boundless confidence and bold scientific extrapolation."

—The New York Times

"Sawyer is Canada's answer to Michael Crichton."

—The Toronto Star

ROBERT J. SAWYER

SHADOWPAW
PRESS

THE
DOWNLOADED

THE DOWNLOADED

By Robert J. Sawyer

The Downloaded is also available as an **Audible Original** with a full cast.

Cover and interior design: **Bibliofic Designs**

Shadowpaw Press
Regina, Saskatchewan, Canada
www.shadowpawpress.com

The publisher gratefully acknowledges the support of Creative Saskatchewan.

Trade Paperback ISBN 978-1-989398-99-9

Printed in Canada

First Edition: May 2024

BOOKS BY ROBERT J. SAWYER

NOVELS

Golden Fleece
End of an Era
The Terminal Experiment
Starplex
Frameshift
Illegal Alien
Factoring Humanity
FlashForward
Calculating God
Mindscan
Rollback
Triggers
Red Planet Blues
Quantum Night
The Oppenheimer Alternative
The Downloaded

The Quintaglio Ascension Trilogy

Far-Seer
Fossil Hunter
Foreigner

The Neanderthal Parallax Trilogy

Hominids
Humans
Hybrids

The WWW Trilogy

Wake
Watch
Wonder

COMPLETE SHORT FICTION

Volume 1: Earth
Volume 2: Space
Volume 3: Time

For book-club discussion guides, visit **sfwriter.com**

DEDICATION

For

Eric Greene

A good and wise ape

ACKNOWLEDGMENTS

As always, Carolyn Clink was the guiding light through this project, one that was created in trying times indeed. Huge thanks to Chris Lotts for structuring a complex deal for this novel, and to Jolise Beaton, Anna Gecan, and dramaturge extraordinaire Gregory J. Sinclair at Audible Canada.

Many thanks to Alisha Souillet, who was my number-one beta reader. Thanks, too, for help from Gregory Benford, Denise Bérubé, Craig Bobchin, Stephanie Bradfield, C.A. Bridges, Matt Campbell, Jon Caruana, Stuart Coxe, Gerald Cuccio, Nancy T. Curriden, Irene Dutchak, Andrew Fink, Paddy Forde, Michael S. Jäger, Herb Kauderer, Mike Lazaridis, W. Thomas Leroux, John Manley, Amanda Potter, N.R.M. Roshak, Alex Shvartsman, Peter Spasov, Lou Sytsma, Douglas Tindal, Gord Tulloch, and Bret Wiebe. I borrowed the term "corpsicle" from my friend Larry Niven.

Many thanks to my Patreon supporters (all of whom had the chance to beta-read this novel) including, most generously, Christopher Bair, Keith Ballinger, Kelly Barratt, Judith Bemis, Jennifer Blanchard, Ronda Bradley, Bill Brooks, Wayne Brown, James Burns, Matt Campbell, Matt Ceccato, James Christie, Phillip Clark, Christine V. Connell, Nancy T. Curriden, Robert M. David, Genevieve Doucette, Allison Dubarry, Hugh Gamble, Gordon Getgood, Joe Karpierz, James Kerwin, Gregory Koch, Archie Kubacki, Matthew LeDrew, Adam Leon, Joel Lee Liberski, Kathe Lopez, Gillian Martin, Catharine McKeever, Cary Meriwether, Lisa Mishchenko, Christina Dawn Monroe, Arioch Morningstar, Kel N., Anna Nelson, Shane P. Newton, The Nolan Family, Andrew Olsen, Carolyn Collins Petersen, Ian Pedoe, Bo Prince, Ken Ray, Carol Richards, Saul Rhymes, Fiona Reid Roma, Rahadyan Timoteo Sastrowardoyo, Robin Schumacher, Timothy W. Spencer, Aaron Suarez, Andrew Tennant, Douglas Tindal, Miss R-Laurraine Tutihasi, Kurt Weingarten, Scott Wilson, Joshua Paul Wolff, Brian Wright, and Len Zaifman.

If you'd like to join them in supporting my work directly, please visit patreon.com/robertjsawyer.

CHAPTER 1

*Any civilization's collapse begins
the moment its people start to ask
themselves "Does this bring me
joy?" rather than "Does this bring
others joy?"*

—James Kerwin

Interview with Dr. Jürgen Haas

So you're the . . . the *person* who wants to interview each of us? I know it's hot out, but you should be wearing a coat, don't you think? A mackinaw? As in *deus ex machina*? Thank you, thank you, I'm here—well, for the next seven years, at least. Try the five-hundred-year-old veal, and don't forget to tip your robot.

Nothing? Crickets? Talk about a tough room! Anyway, yeah, sure, I'm glad to be interviewed. But I bet some of the others will refuse. No, no—not any of us, but some of *them*. Go ahead, though; fire away.

Oh, don't bother calling me "Dr. Haas." "Jürgen" is fine, thanks. What? Sorry; I'm having trouble understanding your accent. When did I first realize something was wrong? Let's see. It was nighttime. Why? Because I *like* nighttime. Heck, sometimes I let the night last for—well, for what seemed like days, if you get my drift.

There was a full moon. In movies, it's *always* a full moon, isn't it? Used to bug the heck out of me. And if they showed a dark night sky, it was just some random spattering of stars, never any recognizable constellations. But I made sure *my* sky was correct: Ursa Major in the north, mighty Orion in the south—although I did cheat on the planets, like they used to in planetariums. Instead of untwinkling points, each showed a small disc. I could see the cloud bands on Jupiter, the rings around Saturn, and hints of geography on Mars.

But, yeah, I guess I like the full moon as much as the next guy, so it usually was full for me. I know the glare should have banished most of the stars, but in the Jürgen-verse the very heavens bent to my will.

A megalomaniac? *Moi?* That'd only be true if they were *delusional* fantasies. But the moon was indeed full and the stars were blazing; even the ones right by the lunar disc were visible, while the Milky Way arched gloriously from horizon to horizon. And, no, there weren't any clouds. I've looked at clouds from both sides now—a perk of the job, see?—and unless they resemble a dragon or something else cool, I've got no use for them.

So, yeah, a *perfect* night sky. All it needed were streamers of northern lights, like in a Yukon tourism ad, and—*voilà!*—there they were: rippling green and gold sheets. Gorgeous. But it wasn't freezing; screw that. It was as warm as an old-time August night in Toronto, but with none of that damn humidity.

Now, a night like that, you gotta do something special, right? Like, say, bodysurf over Niagara Falls. As a kid, I once saw the falls long after sunset, when they lit them up with different colors. My version was like that, too: foaming sheets of pink and magenta, green and teal.

I had the Niagara River raging toward the precipice, a wild torrent, kicking up spray that diffracted the moonlight into rainbows. On the shores were beds of white trilliums, the goddamn provincial flower, which I'd seen precisely *once* in the wild. But they *are* beautiful, so what the heck: millions were as easy as one.

And, sure, body surfing in the dark is *insane*, but that's what made it worth doing. Now, a stunt like that needed an audience, and so I conjured one up: Letitia, dreadlocks down her back, long shapely legs quickly closing the distance between us, a huge, warm smile across her gorgeous face.

Don't look at me like that. She *is* gorgeous, and I am *not* objectifying her. I'm just telling you how I saw her, all right? Give me a break.

Sure, it wasn't the real Letitia. She was off in her own silo just like I was in mine. I hadn't seen her in the flesh for—God, had it really been four years? Time flies when you're having fun—or, I suppose, when your system clock is running fast.

But, actually, the clock there was running *slow*. Yes, from my point of view, just four years had passed in that simulated reality, so it was now 2063 as far as I was concerned, but five *centuries* had slipped by in the outside universe. That made it sometime in the mid-2500s, meaning we should have been getting close to our destination.

The last time I'd seen the real Letitia, she'd been thirty-eight. I was a year older—still am, subjectively—but got my astronaut's wings a year after she did; medical school takes time.

Anyway, there was no need to wear clothes; nothing could hurt me, and the temperature was always whatever I found comfortable. Still, I summoned up a pair of swim trunks in ANSA blue and gold. For her part, Letitia was wearing—well, that was odd. She was in her astronaut's jumpsuit. But at least its light tan color made her visible in the dark.

I looked back to make sure Letitia was paying attention, then braced myself on the trillium-covered north bank—the Canadian side—and bent down in a low crouch, then leapt up, up, up into the air. At the pinnacle, I swung my arms over my head, ready to pierce the raging waters as my trajectory started angling downward. When I hit, the water was warm—no need to suffer, after all!—and I remained submerged for a full minute before rising to the surface, my body sluicing along the top of the frothing river, barreling (but not in a barrel!) toward the sheer cataract of Niagara Falls.

Just before I reached the rocky lip, I realized that I could have even more spectators if I added the *Maid of the Mist* sightseeing boat, with its crowd of tourists clad in yellow slickers, and—*ta-da!*—there it was, up ahead and far below, as I shot over the precipice like I had a booster rocket up my bum. I must have been flying forward ten meters for every one I dropped in altitude, and I soon realized that by the time I hit the Niagara River, Letitia would be far behind.

I've got a silly fondness for superhero movies, so I pulled my right arm back against my body, the way Superman does when executing a turn, and started arcing back toward her. The air whipped my hair and flung moisture from my body. I imagine from Letitia's point of view I was a silhouette against the night, backlit by the moon. To rectify that, I made three spotlights on rotating mounts appear along the south bank and let their beams converge on me as I continued to swoop down toward her.

Letitia should have been applauding wildly and grinning from ear to ear, but she was doing neither. Instead, she just stood there, arms folded across her chest, shaking her head. The system usually knows what I want to see, but I could always override its choices through an effort of will and I made an effort then, telling the Letitia simulation to let out a cheer and then come running toward where I was about to land.

But nothing happened. She just stood there, looking pissed. I spread my arms as though they were brakes and came down gently about three meters from her. As I walked toward her, I noticed something startling. Her dreadlocks were longer than I'd ever seen them, but that didn't bother me; the more the merrier, says I. But from the top of her head down to the middle of her bottom, they were interspersed with red beads, like cranberries strung along twine. Beads I don't mind, but I hate the color red—yeah, strange for a doctor, I know—and there's no way I'd have conjured up a vision of her looking like this.

I blinked rapidly three times—my usual trick for correcting glitches—but nothing changed. "Jesus, Letitia," I said, hearing my own voice for the first time in ages. "That was pure athletic gold right there. Why the resting bitch face?"

Anger shone through her normally charming Jamaican lilt. "I'd forgotten what a little boy you can be, Jürgen. Maybe I should turn to Dr. Chang instead."

Chang. That bastard. One of the best things about going into my own silo had been leaving other people behind—certain ones, at least. "Simulation override phi chi psi omega," I said. "Reset Letitia."

But Letitia remained exactly as she had been, standing among the trilliums, glaring at me. "Conjure up some more clothes, doofus," she said. "We need to talk."

Interview with Captain Letitia Garvey

Yeah, yeah, that's what Jürgen *would* say. Me waiting there for him at the side of the Niagara River with—what did he call it?—"a huge, warm smile" on my face. I won't say it's typically male to cast a woman as a passive spectator, but male astronauts like Jürgen still cling to that macho so-called "right stuff" the original *Mercury* Seven had coursing through their veins. Of course, Jürgen's veins were now filled with antifreeze, like mine, but you know what I mean.

Or maybe you *don't.* I guess I better explain. For me, it started with my grandfather on my mother's side—that's the Jamaican-born one. In 1989, when he was just twenty-nine, he was diagnosed with a rare form of non-Hodgkin lymphoma called mantle cell lymphoma. How rare? Just a few hundred diagnoses a year in North America. How serious? Incurable; terminal. Doctors said he had maybe four years to live.

Well, that wasn't good enough for a man who'd survived a tour of duty as a United Nations peacekeeper. Nor was it good enough for someone who still had what he called his "barrel list," a bucket being much too small to hold all his plans. We had that in common, Gramps and me: a drive to do *everything.* Neither of us could stand it when something got in the way of our goals.

I'd never met him, of course, but Grandma and Mama told me all about him. A black man in what was then the white man's world. He had to fight every step of the way—and so I've got to keep fighting, too, right? Carry on the family tradition.

They used to say a cure for cancer was twenty years in the future—and they'd been saying that for five decades. But they *were* making stumbling progress toward treatments for mantle cell lymphoma back then. There sure as hell wasn't going to be a cure in four years, and maybe not in twenty, but *eventually* there was bound to be one. And so my grandparents decided to have him cryonically frozen when the cancer finally took his life. This was a man who wasn't going to let a little something like stage-four cancer stop him—at least not for good.

Between the life insurance his union job provided and a policy he'd bought separately, there was three million dollars just waiting to be collected—and, back then, that was enough to look after his wife plus my momma-to-be and her two brothers with lots left over for the deep freeze. He signed a contract with ColdBoot, Incorporated, based in Nevada, the world's top-rated cryonics facility.

Ironic, that. Glowing reviews . . . of their grounds, their staff, and their facilities for storing bodies; they had about a hundred and seventy in deep freeze. But no reviews of their ability to resuscitate a dead body, because no one had any idea how to do that. As the joke went, "How many cryonicists does it take to change a light bulb?" "None—they just sit in the dark and wait for the technology to improve."

Well, upon Grandpa's death in 1994, when he was thirty-four, he was indeed frozen. As he said just before he passed away, he was always a chill dude anyway.

During the opening decade of the twenty-first century, treatments for mantle cell lymphoma involving chemotherapy were developed, but they couldn't be called cures. Even if you managed to beat the disease back until there was no trace of it in the body, mantle cell, caused by a chromosomal translocation, had a one-hundred-percent recurrence rate. The fucking thing *always* came back, and the second time it was almost impossible to knock down.

But soon, robust treatments were developed, combining chemo and radiation with an autologous stem-cell transplant. That technique was the gold standard for a while, and usually gave the patient nine or ten years of life following initial diagnosis. And then, in the 2020s, there came something called CAR T-cell therapy. Finally, oncologists started using the word "cure" in relation to this cancer, although the noun was still most often preceded by the adjective "potential."

My grandma missed her husband but was in no rush to have him revived, partly because she was afraid of what a man whose body was still that of an amateur athlete in his thirties would make of a wife who was now a senior citizen.

But by 2032, CAR T had been replaced by advanced genetic techniques, providing a total, permanent cure. And so my grandmother decided it was time. She, my momma and poppa, my uncles Devon and Leroy, and twelve-year-old me converged on Nevada and asked ColdBoot to revive him. It was a historic moment, something Grandpa never could have anticipated when he'd signed up for this: turned out he was the *first* person any cryonics facility anywhere was going to try to bring back to life. They'd have to rapidly remove the antifreeze that had replaced his blood to keep his cells from exploding, fill him up with six liters of O-positive, and then restart his heart.

Grandpa's body, removed from the steel canister that had held it for thirty-eight years, was shrouded in rapid-heating thermal blankets. Wall displays big enough that we could read them from the upstairs observation gallery showed his vital signs, or lack thereof: body temperature was 17°C and rising rapidly, but both his EKG and EEG showed flat lines, as did his respiration monitor; one on me would have revealed the same thing as I held my breath.

There were two more digital readouts, each glowing red, one atop the other. The upper one was labeled "Chronological Age," and said "72 years / 3 months / 22 days." The lower one was marked "Biological Age," and said what you'd have found on Grandpa's death certificate issued almost four decades earlier: "34 years / 10 months / 5 days."

Finally, it was time for the defibrillation. One of the nine doctors in the room pulled back the blankets, and another applied the paddles, and—

—and Grandpa's chest heaved, and the electrocardiogram jumped into action, and, moments later, so did the brain-wave monitor. Just after that, the respiration monitor showed him taking giant shuddering breaths. We watched his chest rise and fall.

I glanced at the biological-age readout and saw that

"days" now showed a six, which was doubtless a bit of theater: having that value arbitrarily set to just before the end of one day so that his new life would be marked by a changing of the last digit.

Up in the gallery, we hugged one another and let out excited whoops. Tears of joy collected in my grandmother's eye sockets. Below, those doctors not immediately occupied were giving each other high-fives or shaking gloved hands. We waited for Grandpa's eyes to flutter open . . .

And we waited.

And waited.

Finally, my mother couldn't take it any longer. In the gallery with us were three ColdBoot executives, and Momma and I turned to face them. "Well? Why hasn't he woken up?"

Mr. Nakamura, a tall man with slicked-back hair, tried for a reassuring smile, but I could tell it was forced. "He's probably just like me: no matter how long I've slept, when the alarm goes off, I want five more minutes."

Momma frowned, but we turned back to look out the angled windows at the revival room. The celebratory atmosphere had evaporated and all nine doctors were hustling about. One flicked his index finger against Grandpa's forehead as if trying to get a piece of machinery with a loose connection to work.

After a couple more minutes it proved too much for Nakamura. He leaned forward and pressed an intercom button mounted on the window sill. "Heather, what's going on down there?"

A doctor with skin even darker than mine looked up and, although the bottom of her face was behind a mask, there was no mistaking the panic in her eyes. "Everything was nominal," she said. "Everything *is* nominal, but . . ."

"Then why isn't he awake?" demanded Nakamura.

Her shoulders lifted and fell in a shrug that mirrored the tracing on the respiration monitor. "I don't know."

Grandpa didn't wake up that day . . . or the next . . . or

the one after that. Finally, Nakamura gathered us all in his office. "I'm so sorry," he said, "but Mr. Henderson is in a coma. He's completely nonresponsive to external stimuli. Everything is working fine, except he isn't conscious."

"You promised you could revive him!" my grandmother said.

"Well, *I* didn't," said Nakamura, who would have been in public school back when Grandpa was frozen, "but he *has* been revived. He's come back to life. No one has ever been resuscitated, and—"

"Fuck that!" said Grandma, the first time I'd ever heard her use such language. "That isn't living."

Nakamura nodded reluctantly. "We're flying in experts in neuroscience—best in the business. Meanwhile, we should discuss . . ."

"What?" said Grandma. "You want more money? Good Christ!"

Nakamura held out his hands palms up. "No, no, no. Of course not. It's just that . . . well, he still has mantle cell lymphoma, and there's nothing about the gene-resequencing cure that requires him to be conscious. I suggest we go ahead and eliminate his cancer so that when he *does* wake up, he'll be healthy."

But he never did wake up. We moved him into a long-term-care facility near Grandma's house in Montego Bay, and she went to visit him every day until she herself passed away.

There'd been funds set aside to freeze her when her time came, but, after watching her beloved just lie there year after year, she chose not to follow in his footsteps. And, really, who could blame her? In the time since ColdBoot had tried to bring Grandpa fully back to life, they'd also tried to revive seven others as cures were found for the things that had killed them . . . and not one had regained consciousness.

ColdBoot's competitors also tried reviving "corpsicles," as the press had taken to calling them, and although in all but one case, in which the body didn't resuscitate at all, the once-dead *did* regain biological activity, they never woke up. Simple old age finally caused Grandpa's revived body, which it seemed had no ghost to give up, to fail. He passed away in 2056, at the age of ninety-five, after spending the last quarter-century just lying there, unresponsive, a fate worse than death.

Eventually, scientists figured out why the cryonics companies couldn't wake up any of their patients. ColdBoot and their ilk had assumed both the body and the mind could be frozen then thawed out as good as new. But while they were refining their techniques for dodging the grim reaper, other companies confirmed what some had suspected since way back in the 1980s. Although the autonomic parts of the central nervous system run purely along classical physics lines, consciousness—the self-reflective inner life—is a product of quantum-mechanical interactions, and it was subject to the usual bane of quantum effects: decoherence. After a few days, the quantum state would collapse, destroying the consciousness that had once existed, and nothing anyone had ever tried managed to regenerate it. All those frozen people might as well have spent far less money on burial plots: they were gone, gone, gone.

Interview with Roscoe Koudoulian

More questions? Christ, I thought I was through with all that. At least you aren't a hostile D.A. who just wants to lock people up. Or maybe you *are*? Seriously, why should I believe you when you say you're not judging us? *Everybody* judges. That's human nature—and, well, I guess that's *your* nature, too, right?

No response? Fine; be that way. Aren't you at least going to ask me what I was in for, though? Isn't that what everybody wants to know when they hear you're an ex-con? Well, I'll tell you. I killed a man. Weasely little asshole tormenting me on social media. Hiding behind a pseudonym. Jerkface thought I'd never figure out who he really was. But it was child's play. I just waited for one of his comments to have a distinctive way of saying something, and eventually on Facebook, he said I was a disgrace to *Homo sapiens*—but he spelled the *sapiens* part so wrong even the automatic speller had no idea what he was trying to say. None of that "I before E except after C" bullshit; he didn't even have an "I" in it. No, he wrote S-A-Y-P-E-U-N-S. So I popped over to Town-Square and put that spelling in the search box to see if anyone there had used it, and Jesus fuck if my jaw didn't drop.

There he was, and with no pseudonym: Mitch Aldershot, the main bully of my childhood, who'd lived the next block over back in West Lafayette. Guy had tracked me down as an adult and decided he wanted to continue to get his jollies by making my life miserable again, I guess. But, like all bullies, he was a coward, hiding behind a phony name. I'd block him, but he'd come back under another name, and then another and another.

Anyhow, now that I finally knew who he was, finding where he lived was easy. He wasn't in Indiana anymore, and neither was I. He'd parked his asswipe self in Boston and I was in Buffalo, but it wasn't long before my business took me to Beantown.

I rented a car at the airport—a completely self-driving one—and rode along, watching the news. I don't remember the exact date, but it was a Saturday afternoon in May or June of '57. You could pin it down, I guess, from the news stories I saw. There was something about that coup in Florida, I think, and the results of the privacy referendum from the Mars colony.

Anyway, the car did a perfect job of parking on the street outside Aldershot's house. My plan, such as it was, had been to march up and push his doorbell. I honestly didn't know if he'd open up for me; he'd be able to see who it was through his doorcam. But when I arrived, he'd apparently just finished mowing his lawn and was returning the mower to his garage, the door to which was up. I almost admired him for a second, doing that chore himself instead of having a robot do it.

I followed him in, the sound of the mower's wheels on the garage floor masking my approach. I hit the button on the wall that I guessed operated the door, and sure enough the hinged panels started coming down.

Mitch swung around, startled. "What the hell?" he said. And then he saw who was in there with him. "Koudoulian?" he spluttered. He knew what I looked like; he'd seen all my online photos—me and my two border collies, me and my daughter on those weekends I had custody of her, me coaching her baseball team.

"Aldershot," I replied, just to make sure he understood that I also knew who he was. Time had certainly turned the tables: I was a good five inches taller than him now and outweighed him by thirty pounds, all of it muscle.

We looked at each other, terror on his face and, I imagine, fury and determination on mine. Off to my left was a doorway that I guessed led into the house. I quickly moved to put myself between him and it.

"What—what do you want?" stammered Aldershot.

The sweetest thing, I thought. *A dish best served cold,* I thought. *A settling of scores,* I thought. But what I said was, "To knock you on your fucking ass."

He raised his hands in a "Be cool, man," gesture, and started backing away, abandoning the lawnmower. I was glad his car wasn't there. We now had an arena bigger than a boxing ring; plenty of room to give him the epic shit-kicking he deserved.

"Look, um, Roscoe," he said. "I never—"

"Never what? Never meant to make my life a living hell? Starting when I was four, for God's sake! Beating the crap out of me day in and day out, for what? Because I sometimes wore a *Star Trek* T-shirt? Because I had a lazy eye? Because I'm left-handed?" I took a step toward him and then another. "I used to wonder what would make someone turn out like you. Some of the other kids said your father beat you. Everyone knew he was a drunk, so maybe he did. But that's only an excuse—if it's any kind of excuse at all—when *you're* a kid yourself. But you tracked me down again, thirty years later. Why, damn it?"

He stayed silent as he shuffled slowly backward toward the rear wall of the garage, which was partially covered by the electric charging station and a Masonite pegboard holding gardening tools.

"*Why?*" I demanded again.

"You're such a wuss, Koudoulian," he said, pulling his favorite childhood insult out of the past.

That did it. I lunged. He darted to one side, but I grabbed his arm, spun him around, and slammed him against the back wall. "Don't call me that," I said, seething. "Don't you ever dare call me that again." I jerked him forward then slammed him back again. Next, I pulled him toward me—and saw that the back of his head had left a bloody mark where it had hit the wall.

"*Why?*" I said, my voice a low rumble. "Why come at me after all these years?"

He turned his head to the left, eyeing the door to the house, but said nothing.

I smashed him against the wall once more, the Rorschach of blood growing larger. He brought up his knee to kick me in the balls—just like he always used to do when beating me up. I twisted to avoid that, and he used the leverage to get away. But I managed to trip him, and he went face-first onto the garage floor. Within seconds, I was looming over him and booted him in the kidneys. "*Why?*" I demanded once more.

He drew up into a fetal position but just grunted. I

kicked him again. "Why?"

"Because . . ." he said between wheezing, wet breaths, "because when I found you online—just curious to see what had become of you, is all—you were posting all kinds of left-wing bullshit, and—"

"You tormented me over *politics?*"

"Bleeding hearts like you have been ruining America for decades. Couldn't have you polluting the mind of that little girl of yours."

What happened next was, as they always say, a blur. I remember whirling around, taking some steps, and grabbing a pair of garden shears from the pegboard. By the time I had them, Aldershot was back on his feet. He ran for the switch that opened the garage door and slammed his palm against it.

I body-checked him into the door as it started to rumble up and I swung him around so he was facing me and—

Yeah, this is the part I don't remember clearly, but I guess the forensics team was right; it probably did happen this way—

I opened the garden shears and drove one of the blades sideways into the middle of his chest. Then I pulled the blade out, and he just stood there, supported only by the slowly rising garage door, his mouth a surprised circle as blood came pouring out of him.

And then, after what seemed like an eternity, the folding panels of the door passed the top of his head, and he tumbled backward and fell onto the driveway . . . just as a woman out walking a poodle passed by on the street. I stood there dumbfounded while she brought out her phone. She must have called 911, because soon enough I heard screaming sirens approaching.

Interview with Captain Letitia Garvey

So, yes, ColdBoot and its competitors could freeze a body, but they couldn't preserve a consciousness. All those decades my Grandpa spent just lying there, he couldn't even be dreaming; everything he had once been was gone for good.

But that didn't stop me from dreaming about him, and when I was in my silo, he was often there with me. Sure, it was a simulacrum, and maybe it really didn't resemble the actual man. Oh, physically, it looked like him; I'd seen enough photos and home movies to get those details right. And I suppose he must have had flaws and foibles like the rest of us, but in *my* reality he was *perfect*. The kind of person I always wanted to be: strong, resourceful, fearless. In my silo, we went adventuring together. I got to relive his peacekeeping experiences, dodging missiles and land mines. And I got to be in Cape Town with him when he went there in 1990 to march with Mandela. In real life, cancer was already slowing Grandpa down by then, and he apparently barely survived a mob attack by a bunch of whites, but in my version I was there with them—him, Mandela, all the others—kicking ass and taking names.

Of course, my grandpa wasn't the only human being who wanted to cheat death. They came along too late for him, but other competing paths toward immortality started to bear fruit, and eventually the notion of scanning and uploading consciousness into a computer went from science fiction—that is, from a rational, reasonable extrapolation of what we actually know—to science fact. Straight digital scanning of a mind accomplished nothing, but using quantum entanglement to produce an exact duplicate inside a quantum computer did the trick.

Except that most of the first quantum copies produced went insane. Why? Because there was nothing for them to see or do inside the quantum computer. They existed but there was no sensory input, no world in which they lived, no space in which they could move.

The first solution tried was slowing the clock speed of the quantum computer to zero; the idea was to store a snapshot of the mind without it experiencing any passage of time. But the same thing happened as with frozen brains: they never rebooted any self-awareness. It turned out that you have to keep consciousness running—and that meant you had to keep it sane, and *that* meant building a virtual-reality environment inside the quantum computer where it could feel and think and interact.

Store the body at sub-zero temperatures; store the mind in a quantum computer—and reunite them at some point in the future. It was a perfect solution not just for those seeking to beat death, like my grandpa, but also for astronauts like Jürgen and me planning to go on a centuries-long interstellar voyage.

Except, damn it all, something went horribly, horribly wrong.

CHAPTER 2

Interview with Roscoe Koudoulian

Damn thing about self-driving cars: of course, the laws vary from state-to-state, but back then in Massachusetts, the cops could send a signal from headquarters that prevented all automobiles in a given area from turning on. They did that as soon as the woman walking by reported Mitch Aldershot's corpse tumbling backward out of his garage as the door rose up revealing me standing there holding the bloody garden shears I'd killed him with.

So, my getaway car was as dead as Mitch Aldershot. Sure I made a run for it, but Boston's finest had no trouble tracking me on street cams, and I was tasered and arrested about three blocks from the scene of the crime.

My eventual trial was pretty open-and-shut on the actual murder rap—that woman had made a video on her phone of the events immediately following Aldershot's death. The big question the jury deliberated about was whether I had premeditated killing him. Weighing against that notion was the fact that I'd shown up at his place with no weapon. But supporting it was the reality that I'd tracked him down, traveled to Boston, and deliberately confronted him with the intent at the very least of assaulting him. That the murder weapon was simply an object at hand—the garden shears—was immaterial asserted the asshole district attorney.

In the end, the jury sided with the state. I was found guilty of first-degree murder and sentenced to fifty years with no possibility of parole for thirty-five.

Thirty-five years. My daughter had turned eight during my trial. That meant she'd be forty-three by the time I got out, probably with children of her own—my grandchildren.

My lawyer, Padma Chopra, said she'd appeal, but, despite what you hear, you don't automatically get another kick at the can. Unless your counsel shows that the judge screwed up somehow, maybe overruling an objection they should have sustained or incorrectly advising the jury on the law, you don't get an appeal—and I didn't.

I'd expected to be hauled off to the state pen, but then something *odd* happened. Instead, Stella Rosen, the head of the Massachusetts Department of Correction, had me and Padma summoned to her office. "Fifty years of hard time," Rosen said as I sat in a chair opposite her clutter-free oak desk.

"Or thirty-five," I countered, "if I get parole."

She leaned back in her swivel chair and interlaced her fingers behind her short graying hair. "True, true. And, for the sake of argument, let's assume you would."

"Bet your ass," I said.

"You've heard about those astronauts who are going to head off to Proxima Centauri?" asked Rosen, a *non sequitur*—a term I'd learned from *Star Trek*—if ever I'd heard one.

"Um, sure."

"They're going to freeze their bodies, putting them into hibernation for the five-hundred-year voyage. And they'll upload their consciousnesses into a quantum computer that'll stay here on Earth, right?"

"I guess."

"Well," continued the director, "we're part of an international pilot project along similar lines, although no one is going to go anywhere in our case. Instead of putting prisoners in a penitentiary, we're giving them the chance to be frozen with their consciousnesses uploaded until their sentences are over. I'm offering you and Ms. Chopra that option."

I'm sure I looked dumbfounded. "Why on Earth would I agree to a bullshit scheme like that?"

"Well, first, the virtual-reality accommodations are much nicer than an actual prison cell. Also, you're in your own silo, as they call them: your own isolated environment. Everybody you interact with will be a simulation rather than a real human being. No need to worry about bullying, prison rape, or anything like that."

"Look at me," I said. "Do I look like I have to worry about bullies?"

"You did at one time, no? That's what brought you here. And you wouldn't believe how many people go to prison thinking they'll be the alpha and come out broken. Yes, you're a murderer, but you're not a career criminal. You have no idea how tough these fuckers can be."

"No sale," I said.

"Wait, let me finish. First, if you agree to participate, your sentence will be reduced to twenty years—that's *better* than getting parole in your case; we want the entire pilot cohort to go in to and come out of their individual virtual prisons simultaneously, so we can study them as a group.

"But the real plus is this: we run the quantum computer holding your consciousness at twenty-four times normal speed. Yes, you'll feel twenty years go by—lots of time to reflect on what you did, and we'll make sure you do that—but only ten months will pass here in the outside world."

"Ten months," I repeated softly.

"That's right—and your frozen body won't have aged a day during that time. You won't come out of prison an old man but still a vigorous guy in his thirties."

I thought about my daughter Annabelle. I could serve my sentence and still be out before she turned ten. Instead of her having to listen to decades of people telling her what a monster her father was without me around to explain, I'd be there with her as she grew up. Her first days in Scouts, her first days in middle school, her first date . . . and the boy or girl better get her home on time!

Padma spoke, surprising me with an unexpected area of expertise: "I didn't think you could speed up simulated reality that much—not and still have high-resolution rendering."

"Ah, yes," said Rosen. "You're right: computers simulating immersive reality usually operate at slower-than-normal clock speeds, not faster ones. But that's because a user can suddenly decide to change locale to, say, a forest in Madagascar, and all of that has to be rendered from scratch, which takes a lot of time and processing resources. But our project deals with people who have, by definition, been deprived of their freedom of movement. We only have to simulate an unchanging prison cell and a couple of other places, and we've already rendered those in high definition. Speeding up the system clock works just fine for our limited purposes."

"Screw all that," I said. "I don't get *why* you'd do this. What's in it for the state?"

Rosen leaned forward. "Simple economics. This costs a tiny fraction of what it does to imprison someone for decades. No food needed, no guards—and my criminologists believe we're much more likely to get a rehabilitated ex-convict out of the process."

"What are the risks?" asked Padma.

"A specialist will take you and your client through a detailed informed-consent process. And, yes, there's always the possibility that something will go wrong. That said, the chance of dying undergoing this procedure is less than a quarter of that of dying a violent death during a thirty-five-year prison term—and there's zero chance of you dying of old age after being frozen for only ten months."

"I'll have to think about it," I said.

The woman smiled, but it was a mirthless grimace. "Of course. We can have you moved into Cedar Junction until you make up your mind."

And those were my two choices: go straight into a state penitentiary or give this crazy plan a try. There was no third scenario in which I got to go home, got to collect one more hug from Annabelle, got to sleep one more night in my own bed.

I looked at Padma, who lifted her hands in an "it's up to you" way, then I turned back to Rosen. "All right," I said. "Count me in."

Interview with Dr. Jürgen Haas

Where were we? Oh, yeah. You'd asked me when I first realized that things had gone to ratshit. Well, it's like I said: there we were, standing on the shore of the Niagara River, me glistening from my bravura display of body surfing and Letitia glaring at me.

She told me to put on more clothes—she's no fun—and so I imagined myself wearing what had been typical garb for me before uploading: tennis shoes, tan denim jeans, and an orange floral-print Hawaiian shirt.

And that was the first sign something was amiss, see? This hard-nosed woman in front of me was, somehow, the *real* Letitia, not the avatar of her I'd dreamed up. "How the hell did you get in here?" I demanded.

"You mean in your private silo? Despite what you seem to think, Jürgen, I'm more than just a pretty face. I'm captain of the mission, remember? I have access privileges that others don't. Damn good thing, too, because something has gone very wrong."

"What?"

"You know what day it is?"

I figured I had a one-in-seven shot. "Tuesday."

"No, no. I mean the date—the objective date in the outside world."

"Well, um, I guess it's 2540 . . . something . . . by now, right?"

She shook her head, stunned that I hadn't been paying attention to the calendar. "It's February fourteenth, 2548."

"Oooh! And you wanted to see me for Valentine's Day!"

A frown. "No, numbnuts. That's the day, according to the mission timer, on which I'm supposed to check the external cameras as we begin our final approach to Proxima Centauri b. Just to make sure it's safe to send our landing craft down, right?"

"Right. And?"

"And you know what the cameras showed, big and bright as your fat ass?"

I shook my head.

She pointed at an upward angle. "That."

I turned and looked, and there it was, lovely and full. "A moon?" I said.

"Not just *a* moon," she replied. "*The* moon. Our moon. Luna."

"How the hell did our moon get to Proxima Centauri?"

She looked at me like I was an idiot. "It didn't. We never went there. Funny thing: the moon is way easier to recognize than Earth; all those clouds obscure Earth's geography. When I first saw Earth, I assumed I was looking at Proxima b—a beautiful, perfect home for us—but there's no mistaking our moon. It wasn't full, like your fake one here; I watched it for an hour, and you could see it visibly getting more gibbous. The Seas of Tranquility and Serenity were obvious, not to mention Tycho and its rays. There's no question: our starship is still in orbit around Earth."

"That can't be right," I said.

"It is! It is. We're *not* almost to another star; we haven't even left on our journey yet. We've spent five centuries going nowhere."

"Jesus," I said.

"But that's not the worst of it. I mean, if that's all that had gone wrong, I could just fire up the *Hōkūleʻa*'s engines and send us on our way. Yeah, it'd be four more subjective years until we reached Proxima Centauri, but so what? It's not like our bodies are aging."

That sounded fine to me; I'd been having a blast. "Okay."

"No, it's *not* okay. Because I also tied into the shipboard cameras and checked the hibernation bay. And guess what? It's empty. Our cryo-coffins were never loaded on board."

"So where are they? Where are our bodies?"

"Who in the hell knows? But there's one way to find out. If I don't override anything, the mission profile calls for you and me to be reintegrated—bodies revived and minds downloaded back into them—in about two hours."

As the *Hōkūleʻa*'s physician, I was supposed to revive along with the captain, to help in case anything went wrong with the automated reanimation of the others. "Have you tried contacting Mission Control?" I asked.

"Of course. No answer. In fact, I can't pick up *any* radio signals."

"So the *Hōkūleʻa*'s communications system has failed," I said, preferring to suggest that possibility rather than any of the darker ones roiling my thoughts.

"Apparently," said Letitia. "So, are you game? Like I said, I can prevent you from downloading, but there *should* be a doctor along."

I'm sure I frowned. A lot could happen in five centuries. There was no guarantee if we downloaded into a bad situation that the equipment still existed to upload our consciousnesses again. And, well, I *loved* my private silo; I'd gotten quite used to that life. I suppose that's why I hadn't been keeping track of the date; I wasn't looking forward to our arrival. Yeah, I'd fought tooth-and-nail to be selected for the Proxima Centauri mission—chief medical officer on the U.N.S.S. *Hōkūleʻa*, Earth's first starship!—but that was years ago.

And the twenty-four of us in the crew were all of the same type. We didn't have family ties in the real world; that's one reason we'd been willing to head off to Proxima Centauri to establish a colony there. We'd never intended to set foot on Earth again. And, now, if we did, five hundred years after we'd been frozen, we'd probably be freaks—like those pathetic bastards who'd signed up with ColdBoot would be if they were ever revived.

As I stood there looking at Letitia, I was getting tired of the roar of the Niagara River and the darkness, so, with a snap of my simulated fingers, I switched us to a quiet forest in autumn, a carpet of red, orange, and yellow maple leaves beneath my feet. It was just one of the countless places both real and imagined that I could conjure up at will—while I was still in here. But if I downloaded all my superpowers would disappear.

"You know what?" I said. "I think I'll pass." Letitia's mouth dropped open, and I held up a hand. "Look," I continued, "no matter where we are, we're in no danger. If something was going to go wrong with the hibernation equipment or the quantum computer, it would have happened long ago. And I assume the rest of our crew are all as happy as I was until a few minutes ago. Given that the Proxima mission was aborted for some reason, what's the point of calling any of us back from our individual versions of heaven?"

"Well, *I'm* going to download," Letitia said firmly. "Heaven is all well and good—mine had lots of horses to ride and new lands to tame, not to mention plenty of loved ones and good company—but it's my responsibility to find out what went wrong. But, okay, if you're unwilling, I'll get Dr. Chang to come with me instead."

I kind of liked that notion: Chang, the prick, screwed out of his heaven, whatever depraved sort of place *that* might be. Still, she was looking at me with palpable disappointment. There was no exit for her to march out of, no door to slam behind her. She just disappeared—*poof!*

I stood there under the canopy of skeletal branches, flaming leaves all around me. My simulated heart was pounding and there was a knot in the pit of my simulated stomach. It's not that I was chicken, or anything, and, I know, I *had* signed a contract to do my job, but . . .

Suddenly, *poof!*, she was back, arms again crossed in front of her chest. "Is this what you would have done at Proxima Centauri?" she demanded. "Crawled back into your silo the first time a problem came our way? That's not the Jürgen I know."

The words stung, but she *was* right; it wasn't the Jürgen *I* knew, either. Heaven, it seemed, changed a man . . . into something perhaps a little less than he'd been before. I considered for a time, then said words I'd never thought I'd say: "Computer, end program." The forest primeval faded away leaving nothing but my avatar and Letitia's floating in a vast grayness, an empty void I imagine was like the one blind people describe living in.

"All right," I said at last. "All right, damn it all. Let's go find out where the hell we are."

Interview with Captain Letitia Garvey

Yes, indeed, copy that. This timing stuff can be very confusing. See, there was never going to be any relativistic time dilation on our journey; the starship *Hōkūleʻa*'s maximum velocity is only about one percent of the speed of light. The difference between the time our minds experienced within the quantum computer and the time that passed outside was entirely due to the computer's clock running at just 1/120th of normal speed. For every year that passed outside only three days went by for us. That was supposed to make our interstellar journey seem like a tolerable four years instead of five centuries, get it?

And, yeah, our consciousnesses were always supposed to stay here on Earth; there was much less chance of them decohering here than during a long, radiation-filled space voyage. Quantum entanglement operates instantly over even infinite distances, so there was no reason our minds couldn't eventually be reunited with our bodies aboard the ship once it reached Proxima Centauri.

But all that was likely moot now: since our bodies hadn't been loaded aboard the *Hōkūleʻa*, then they were probably still here on Terra Firma. Clearly, something was hugely wrong, and I girded myself for the worst, prepared to deal with whatever Jürgen and I would find—if the revival of our bodies and the downloading worked, that is. Jürgen's stunt of body surfing over Niagara Falls was nothing compared to this leap of faith. Shit was about to get real.

It takes about twenty minutes to heat up a frozen body, refill it with blood, and defibrillate it—but that was real-world time. Those twenty minutes flashed by in just ten seconds for us.

And then the automatic downloading began. Although our avatars were full-body representations, they were just window dressing for the consciousnesses kept intact inside the quantum computer. The visual effects as our minds moved from in there back into our now-revived bodies were simply the artifice of some long-dead programmer. But it was cool to watch as Jürgen dissolved from the feet up, while, I suppose, the same thing was happening to me. Soon, his legs were gone, and then the bottom of his torso—which, I imagined, increased his intelligence—then his upper torso, and . . .

And then, just like that, I was back in a real flesh-and-blood body, staring up at a real ceiling, with real LED lighting fixtures in it. I felt itchy and my head hurt and so did my back and my throat was dry and the light was stinging my eyes and, oh my God, it was *wonderful.*

Interview with Dr. Jürgen Haas

Letitia and I were supposed to download simultaneously into our revived bodies, but I guess the transference of my mind started a fraction of a subjective second prior to hers—which meant, thanks to the quantum computer's slowed clock, I woke up in the real world several minutes before she did.

My cryo-coffin had opened already, which was a good thing—it would have been scary as hell to transfer into the absolute darkness of a sealed container. There were four ports surgically attached to my body: one going into each of my femoral arteries and one apiece into my carotids. Through them, the antifreeze had already been sucked out and my own blood, stored in a reservoir in the coffin's base, had been pumped back in. I undogged the flexible tubes going into those ports, wondering why there wasn't a doctor here to do that for me.

I lay there for a time, feeling an enormous sense of loss—like I'd just been swindled out of everything I held dear. I was almost afraid to sit up and see more of this . . . this *banal* thing called reality, but, at last I did.

I felt woozy, and there was that sort of white fog in my vision you get when you stand up too quickly, even though I was still sitting. I hadn't had a headache, or *any* ache, all the time I'd been in my silo.

I recognized the surroundings immediately: the hibernation chamber at the Quantum Cryonics Institute. Letitia was right: our bodies hadn't gone anywhere; they were still on Earth. The chamber didn't have any windows, but the lights were on; I wondered if they'd been on for the past five centuries or had lit up in response to my reanimation procedure.

Five centuries.

Or was it? I mean, sure, that had been the plan, but . . .

"Hello, Dr. Haas," said a male voice. My heart jumped—a real, beating, blood-pumping heart. I swung my head and there, beside my coffin, was a squat robot with black loco-motor treads, a steampunk-looking boxy torso, and a brick-shaped head. It took me a moment to remember his name. "Penolong?"

"Yes, indeed," replied the robot, his glassy front eyes fixed on me. "I know it can take a long time to get to see a doctor," he continued, "but making me wait five hundred years is a bit much, don't you think?"

And there it was: confirmation. Still, to be sure, I asked Penolong the date. He replied with the same one Letitia had earlier: "Fourteen February 2548." And then, although it seemed much less funny now than when I'd said something similar, he added, "Happy Valentine's Day."

Penolong had been an assistant to the doctors who'd su-pervised the suspending of our life functions and the freez-ing of our bodies. I was about to ask what had happened to Megan, who'd been the head of that team, but she must be long dead. Still, I said, "Where is everybody?"

"I don't know," Penolong replied. "Once you lot were frozen, I deactivated myself until just now, when I might be needed again."

"Huh," I said. "A robotic Rip van Winkle." A wall clock displayed 8:42, but I had no idea if it was a.m. or p.m.

"Here," said Penolong, moving on his revolving treads around to the other side of my coffin, "let me help you get out." He was much shorter than me, but his mechanical arms were strong, and I used them as a brace as I hauled myself over the rim and onto my feet. Dizzy, I held onto him for support.

I was naked, of course, but, unlike back in my silo, were I was usually naked, I felt vulnerable and exposed—as well as cold. I gestured toward the hermetically sealed footlocker at the end of my cryochamber. "My clothes still in there?" I asked.

"I'll see," said Penolong. I let go of him and switched to holding on to the rim of the coffin. He moved over to the locker—which was misnamed, as it had no actual lock—opened it, and brought me my astronaut jumpsuit, underwear, socks, and shoes.

As I struggled to get dressed, dealing with such real-world indignities as a sock snagging on a sharp corner of my big toenail, I said, "Captain Garvey should be reviving, too. Where is she?"

The cryo-coffins were arranged in four rows of six, each unit about two meters from the next. Penolong rolled over to the first row and stopped by Letitia's coffin. "Here," he said.

I was still unsteady and had to grab onto other units as I made my way over to join him. Just as I was arriving, the metal lid on Letitia's coffin split down its length, emitting a cloud of frigid nitrogen, and the two halves descended into the unit's sides, revealing her earthly remains, covered by the thermal blanket.

I thought about looming over her, so that the first sight she'd see when she opened her eyes would be my smiling face, but I decided not to. She deserved the same sort of private moments I'd just had, coming to grips with being physical again. I gestured for Penolong to follow me and we moved to the foot of her coffin, where I could watch the status panel detailing her reanimation. For support, I leaned my crooked right elbow on Penolong's head.

Soon enough, Letitia was stirring. I stepped forward, in case she needed a hand, but she was doing better than I had and was already sitting up. She gave me a little wave, and Penolong said, "Welcome back, Captain Garvey."

The thermal blanket had slipped down revealing her naked torso—looking *fine* for someone who was 528 years old—but she quickly did as I had done, asking for her clothes. Penolong opened her footlocker and fetched them, and I confess I enjoyed watching her stretch and bend as she put them on. When she was dressed, she glanced around and nodded, presumably to herself; she no doubt recognized where we were, too. But then her eyes went wide. "What the fuck?" she said.

I turned to look where she was looking but didn't see what she was referring to—not at first. "Yes?" I said.

Her voice was raw and dry, but the words were unmistakable. "Why are there *two* other open coffins?"

She was right. There was mine—and there was another one in the fourth row that was open, too. No one was supposed to be revived before the captain and me.

"My goodness!" said Penolong, and he motored over to check it out.

I staggered over to that unit, too, and when I got there, I said softly, "Oh, God."

That got Letitia moving. Like me, she was still unsteady on her feet, but it was only a few seconds before she joined us, and we all just stared down at what was in front of us.

The coffin hadn't been opened. It had been *smashed,* its cover broken. And inside was a desiccated corpse, the skull staved in and most of the flesh eaten away. There wasn't enough of a face left for me to recognize who this had been.

Letitia looked at the name on the status display. "Mikhail Sidorov," she said, and her voice cracked, whether because her vocal cords were still warming up or because of emotion I couldn't say. Mikhail was our ship's roboticist, responsible for the dozens of robots already loaded into the cargo hold of the *Hōkūle'a* that had been going to help us till the soil and do other manual labor or risky tasks if we'd ever gotten to Proxima Centauri.

I looked up to see if something had fallen from the ceiling onto Mikhail's coffin, but there was no sign of that. And then I looked down and saw it: the crowbar that had presumably been used to open the unit up and smash his skull.

Letitia was clearly as shaken as I was. "Not *quite* murder, is it?" she said. "I mean, presumably Mikhail's consciousness is still intact inside his own silo, but . . ."

"But he can never download into the real world again," I supplied.

"We should see if any of the others have been vandalized," Letitia said. I checked the closest two rows, accompanied by Penolong, while Letitia inspected the two farther ones. All the other units seemed fine.

"Poor Mikhail's been dead for years," I said. "Centuries, maybe. Where the hell is the staff?"

"Do you know?" Letitia asked Penolong.

"No. As I told Jürgen, I've only just woken up myself."

"Let's find out," said Letitia, and she marched—her commander's bearing overcoming any residual wobbliness—toward the door that led out of the cryochamber. I followed her and Penolong followed me. We came into an empty celery-colored corridor. It had been four years, subjectively, since either Letitia or I had been here, and I guess we were both disoriented. "Where are the elevators?" she asked.

"This way," said Penolong, and he rolled on ahead of us. I recalled we were on the second floor, but Penolong couldn't use stairs, so once a lift arrived, the three of us piled into it.

We were deposited on the ground floor but had to go through an airlock-type affair to get into the lobby proper. This whole building was a series of interconnected Faraday cages, with the walls containing meshes of conducting material—necessary to prevent outside electromagnetic interference from causing decoherence in the quantum computers.

The spacious lobby was devoid of people—but not of robots like Penolong; I caught sight of two more such machines, although they seemed indifferent to our presence.

The building's entrance was glass but there was so much glare from sunlight pouring in that we couldn't immediately make out what was outside. It wasn't until we were right up by the floor-to-ceiling window next to the main sliding doors that we finally saw the real world.

"My goodness," Penolong said again as my pulse started racing and my stomach muscles clenched.

Outside, everything was in ruins, overgrown by vegetation. Concrete slabs were tilted at wild angles and they were broken through by massive tree roots. A few rusted heaps that might have once been cars were visible, along with stretches of cracked asphalt, and there were remains of buildings, some completely collapsed, some with their roofs caved in, most with windows smashed. There wasn't a soul in sight.

We were quiet for a time, and then Letitia spoke softly. "I think," she said, "that we're all going to come to envy Mikhail Sidorov. At least he'll never have to return to *this*."

CHAPTER 3

Interview with Roscoe Koudoulian

Before I'd agreed to this crazy scheme of serving my prison sentence in cryosleep, Stella Rosen, the head of the Massachusetts Department of Correction, had said, "Yes, you'll feel twenty years go by—lots of time to reflect on what you did, and we'll make sure you do that—but only ten months will pass here in the outside world."

I hadn't really paid attention to her little aside there: "lots of time to reflect on what you did, and we'll make sure you do that." I was way more interested in getting out in less than a year of real time, missing only one of my daughter Annabelle's birthdays instead of twenty of them.

But the part about making sure I reflected on my crime turned out to be a big fucking deal. You ever see *A Clockwork Orange?* Yeah, yeah, it's an ancient flick, sure, but every old-movie buff like me has seen all of Stanley Kubrick's films, just like we've seen all of Hitchcock's and Welles's and Kerwin's. In that movie, a vicious rapist named Alex was given aversion therapy by being made to watch scenes of sexual violence with his eyelids held open by clamps. It's so disturbing, I gotta say, that it's the only Kubrick film I've only ever watched once.

Well, they didn't *quite* do that with me. But once every subjective week, on every one of the thousand Wednesdays I was in the can, I was "transported" out of my simulated prison cell and dumped into a VR recreation of that day back in 2057 when I'd confronted my childhood bully, Mitch Aldershot, in the garage of his house in Boston. There'd been no actual video of the murder itself—just the immediate aftermath caught on her phone's camera by that woman who'd been walking by with her poodle—but, between my testimony and the CSI team's reconstruction, they did a painfully accurate job of simulating the, ah, event.

Each time I had to relive it, they varied it slightly. Sometimes, I saw it from my point-of-view, the way you would in a first-person shooter. Other times, it was from Aldershot's perspective. Still others, I saw it as if my eyeball had been on the tip of the blade of the garden shears I'd plunged into his chest, past his ribs, and into his heart as it beat its last.

Over and over, again and again. They didn't have to physically pry my eyelids open, the way Alex the droog's had been. When you're an avatar, thems that's running the simulation can control your body parts.

For Alex, they'd played his favorite composer, Beethoven, over the videos he had to watch. I didn't get any musical soundtrack—just the sounds of the fight between me and Mitch, the grunts, the body slams, and, amplified, the tearing of flesh and the beating, and the halting, of his heart.

Cruel and unusual punishment, you say? Maybe so. But it worked, damn it all. It worked. They'd found a way to quell the raging spirit that dwelled within me. Oh, I don't say that if provoked I wouldn't fight back, but the idea of *initiating* violence became, bit by bit, replay by replay, increasingly abhorrent to me.

They tested that over the two virtual decades of my original sentence. I wasn't alone in prison, after all—that *would* have been cruel and unusual punishment. There were a whole bunch of simulated criminals in there with me, and I'm sure Stella and her team of shrinks watched from outside, in the real world, as my ways of dealing with the other cons shifted.

Those simulated felons had clearly been programmed by one of my fellow bleeding hearts. Each was guilty but always with some extenuating factor: a bad upbringing, an incompetent lawyer, a noble necessity for committing their crime. As good as the programmer had been, though, the conversations with these others became repetitive as the years went by. Fortunately, once in a while, one of them got paroled and some new simulation took his place.

Yeah, *his* place. As progressive as this made-up prison was, it was still segregated by gender. If you're straight like me, two decades is a long time to go without ever laying eyes on a woman.

Still, I gotta say, in a way, the real prison officials, whoever they were in the outside world, were downright *kind*. I was supposed to be in the slammer for twenty subjective years, right? Well, apparently just before I uploaded, they'd gotten Annabelle's best friend Avery to wear a bodycam while the two of them went about their adventures for a couple of days—a day of school, with a softball match after, and a Saturday out and about.

And then some decent soul had edited ten half-hour segments from that, picking out the highlights. And they'd programmed the computer running the simulation to pump one of those thirty-minute jewels into my silo every week—every *outside* week, that is, which meant I only got a new one every six *inside* months. But, still, I lived for each new video, and, in between them, they let me replay the old ones as often as I wished.

Annabelle was just about the cutest little girl you ever saw. Yeah, yeah, I'm biased—but it was true. And she was so bubbly, so affectionate, just an absolute joy, the only good thing that had come out of my brief marriage to Darlita. I wanted to hug her, to tousle her dark hair, to play catch with her, to help her with her homework. But I couldn't do any of that; all I could do was look and listen, to laugh when she laughed, to feel my heart bursting with pride when she hit a homer in the softball game, to see her raise her hand and give the right answers about Roman numerals in class—and to cry when the video ended, knowing half a year would pass before I got the next one.

> *"Daddy, Daddy, watch this! Look!*
> *I can do a back flip! See? See? I'll*
> *do it again! There! Cool, huh?*
> *"I'm going to miss you so much*
> *when you go away, Daddy! Don't*
> *be gone too long, 'kay? I love you!"*

God, I miss her. I miss her every single day.

How did I fill my time in prison? They only let us—I say "us" as if the other cons were real people, but of course, they weren't. Anyway, they only let us watch a movie once a week, but we could read as much as we wanted. Well, like I said, I love old movies, and one of my favorites is *The Maltese Falcon*—the Bogart version, that is. I love the novel, too, and I probably read it a half-dozen times during my sentence. John Huston was nominated for an Oscar for best adapted screenplay just for using Dashiell Hammett's dialog from that book word-for-word. In both the movie and the novel, Lieutenant Dundy says to Sam Spade, who he suspects murdered his own partner, "You know me, Spade. If you did or you didn't you'll get a square deal out of me, and most of the breaks."

And most of the breaks. That's the way it's always been, as far as I can tell: whether you have an easy time dealing with the law or a hard one comes down to the whims of the people in power. And I'd believed what Stella Rosen had said. She promised it'd feel like twenty years would go by for me, but only ten months would pass outside.

If twenty real years had gone by, my previous education would have been totally obsolete, but there was no danger of that in only ten actual months. Still, my sentence *did* require me to undergo vocational training. After all, my employer had no obligation to take back a convicted murderer, nor were there many others who'd likely hire one. There weren't many violent offenders who had a master's degree, like I did; mine was a low-residency MBA, with an emphasis on sales and marketing. I had to laugh at that: both my degree and my prison sentence required hardly any time away from home.

Or so they'd said.

Six years. Seven Years. Eight.

I studied how to start my own online business so I wouldn't have to worry about finding someone to give me a job when all this was over. But that was simple and it left me lots of time to explore other things. Without really planning it, I found myself gravitating toward sociology. My father had been a professor at Purdue, and that's what he'd taught. But he was so volatile, so short-tempered—yeah, the apple doesn't fall far, does it?—just about anything could lead to him storming away from the dinner table; I never talked to him about his work or much of anything else.

Ten years. Eleven. Twelve.

There was some irony here, too. One reason Mitch Aldershot used to beat me up—as if a monster like him really needed a justification for nastiness—was that my father was an intellectual, whereas his dad actually *worked,* in construction. I suppose I should have counted my blessings: my dad only hurt with his words; Aldershot's old man used to regularly pound the shit right out of him.

Anyway, I thought maybe I could gain some sort of insight into my father by learning a bit about the subject that had consumed his professional life. And, I gotta say, the more I read about it, the more interesting I found it. From Durkheim, Marx, and Weber through to the present, the notion that one could make sense of masses of humans and, indeed, try to engineer better ways for them to live together, was fascinating. And even more fascinating, to me, was why none of the systems these learned men and women proposed ever seemed to *work*. What the hell was wrong with humanity?

Sixteen years. Seventeen. Eighteen.

At last, the magic date rolled around: the end of my sentence, the day I would be dumped back into my revived body, the day I'd get to go home and see my daughter Annabelle again.

I expected the warden avatar to show up and start the ball rolling, but he never did. I checked with my favorite guard to make sure I hadn't misread the calendar, but of course I hadn't. I waited and waited, and when the day ended, I was still in fucking prison.

The next day, I complained to the guard who supervised the morning roll call—a ridiculous ritual given I was the only real person here—that I was supposed to get out yesterday.

"I'd thought so, too," said the guard.

"Can't you speak to the warden?"

"I will," he replied.

But that day passed by—and the next, and the next.

You'll get a square deal out of me, and most of the breaks.

Damn it, I trusted them!

Twenty-one years. Twenty-two. Twenty-three . . .

Jesus fucking Christ.

Interview with Captain Letitia Garvey

Yeah, so Jürgen and I stared out the lobby windows for a long time. There was no doubt about where we were: the Quantum Cryonics Institute in Waterloo, Ontario, Canada. It was one of the many quantum-science facilities that gave Waterloo its nickname "Quantum Valley."

The building we were in was in good shape, but outdoors everything was ruined. And yet I recognized the shattered structures: the old Bleaney Systems office tower to the left, with a Tim Hortons on the ground floor; what had been a luxury condo tower next to it. There was no futuristic architecture. Whatever had destroyed the city must have occurred shortly after we'd uploaded.

"You suppose it was a nuclear war?" asked Jürgen.

That'd been my first thought, as well—everyone in the middle of the twenty-first century had lived in fear of such a thing. But I shook my head. "Don't think so. Otherwise, this building would be damaged, too." I gestured outside. "That looks like *neglect*. Like everyone died, and so no upkeep was done for centuries."

Jürgen made a *hmmph* sound. "A plague, then?"

"Maybe," I replied then turned to Penolong. "How come this building still has power and lights?"

"The entire rooftop is covered with solar panels," the robot said. "We are energy self-sufficient. It was considered a legal necessity when we started storing bodies and uploading people's minds here. There are cisterns in the courtyards for collecting rainwater, which is processed in the basement. And although I've been deactivated for the past 489 years, you may have noticed that some of my brethren were not; they have done the necessary maintenance and repairs to keep everything functioning."

"Is it safe to go outside?"

"I have no idea," said Penolong, and it pointed at its treads, which would be useless on that topsy-turvey landscape of broken concrete and thick vegetation. "I've never been."

"Shouldn't one of you robots have revived us as soon as it was apparent something had gone wrong?" asked Jürgen.

Penolong put its mechanical hands where its hips would have been if it'd had legs, and I half-expected the machine to retort, "It's not all about you, you know." But its programmers clearly hadn't been experts in human body language because its reply was apologetic not defiant. "I'm sorry, Jürgen. No one but the ANSA liaison has that authority."

"But the liaison must have died centuries ago," Jürgen said.

"Be that as it may," replied Penolong.

Jürgen made an exasperated sound, but I just nodded. "Okay," I said. "First things first." I looked around, but it *had* been four subjective years since I'd been here. "Take us to the operations center for the quantum computer."

Penolong started rolling along and Jürgen and I followed. We went up the same elevator as before, and then the little robot led us along a corridor to the double-pocket metal doors of the operations center. At a signal from the robot, the doors slid aside and interior lighting snapped on. We went in.

The room looked like most computer centers did since the great privacy revolt of the 2040s. Instead of having terminals hooked up to the cloud, all the computing power here was local; a conventional computer of almost infinite capacity could be packed into an arbitrarily small container. The ones that ran this place were squat discs the size of hockey pucks that vaguely resembled the old-fashioned digital assistants they had supplanted.

Along one wall there was a giant monitor currently displaying a diagram of the twenty-four cryo-coffins. Jürgen's and mine were properly shown as empty, and Mikhail Sidorov's was festooned with warning lights. The other twenty-one had green lights, indicating they were operating properly.

The opposite wall was mostly window, overlooking the quantum computer in the next room. Moore's Law hadn't caught up with these marvels yet, and this device, a tetrahedron with perfect silver-gray mirror-like sides, filled its chamber.

Jürgen stood next to me, and we just stared for a long moment. That's where our consciousnesses had been housed these last four subjective years; that's where the minds of the other twenty-two would-be star travelers were still housed, including poor Mikhail's. That's where every bit—every *qubit*—

of our reality had existed, from Jürgen's Niagara Falls to the Jamaica, South Africa, and Himalayas I'd spent time in. My face was being reflected back at me from one triangular side of the tetrahedron, and my expression was something I'd never seen in a photo of myself: simple, unadulterated awe.

I turned and walked to the workstation that controlled the clock speed for the quantum computer. The hockey puck there was a lovely teal color. I sat, tapped a couple of times on its upper surface to get its attention, and spoke. "Login: Letitia Garvey."

"Hello, Letitia," replied the puck. "Long time no see."

"I want to reset the system clock for the quantum computer to—"

"*Countermand,*" said Penolong. I swung to face the robot. It continued: "I can't let you mess about with that. If the system clock glitches, all the stored consciousnesses might decohere."

I blew out air. Penolong stood there, arms dangling loosely from carbon-fiber shoulders—again, utterly the wrong body language for the defiant demeanor it was trying to project.

"*Penolong,*" I said, reining in my anger, "clearly something has gone wrong. Dealing with that is the reason Jürgen and I came out of suspension. You have to let me do this."

"Sorry, ma'am," said the robot, "but I can't allow it."

"You must know that this facility has been abandoned."

"Be that as it may," Penolong said again.

"Look," I said, "I need to contact the other astronauts. But the quantum computer they're living in is running at just 1/120th of normal speed. I can't talk to them if a minute of my words flash by in half a second for them—or if a minute of them talking is stretched out over two hours for me."

"I understand your problem," the robot replied, "but I can't allow you to—what are you doing? Stop!"

Jürgen had clearly had enough. He'd grabbed the little robot by the sides of its boxy torso and had picked it up.

Penolong's treads whirred, but they couldn't do anything. Jürgen carried Penolong right out of the operations center, with the machine protesting, "Put me down! Put me down!" I smiled: sometimes it *did* pay to have the big ape around. I rapped the teal puck again. "Now," I said. "Where were we?"

Interview with Jameela Chowdhury

Wait just a bleeding minute, old boy! You really expect me to tell you everything I know? Might one enquire as to precisely what you're planning to *do* with that information?

Come again? Apologies, but your accent is giving me some difficulty. "Just collecting data," is it? That's what they *all* say! And, no, I don't care one whit that the others have all spoken to you freely. I'm not like them.

Yes, I *do* mean the other astronauts; I'm not like them. Hedonistic bastards, the lot.

My job? I suppose it won't hurt to tell you what you could have looked up on Wikipedia—if Wikipedia still existed, that is. I'm an astrophysicist, with a PhD from Cambridge. My specialty is red dwarf stars.

Right, exactly: Proxima Centauri is a red dwarf, and such stars are notoriously volatile. That's ostensibly why they wanted me along, see? They claimed to need a boffin like me for the mission there.

No, I don't think I will explain what I mean by that—not unless you give me something in return: a little *quid pro quo.* Tell me what Letitia and Jürgen told you about the nature of our mission.

Ah, I see. They're sticking to that story, then. Bleeding typical. And I suppose you believed it, what with their fancy titles: *Captain* Garvey and *Doctor* Haas.

Of course I know better! It's all rubbish. Oh, certainly, the main strokes are correct: the starship *Hōkūle'a* never went anywhere, and almost five hundred years did pass in the outside world while just four years slipped by for us astronauts. But the vaunted Captain Garvey having no idea that her ship hadn't left on its interstellar voyage? Bollocks! And that worldwide competition to join the first mission to another star? A ruse to get us—the best humanity had to offer, if I may be so cheeky—to agree to this rum business of being frozen and uploaded. But it was *not* so we could colonize some far-off planet, but rather so we could repopulate the Earth if a disaster happened . . . as, quite obviously, it has.

How'd I suss it out, I bet you want to know, eh? Well, instead of tuning out the real world, as I'm sure the rest of the crew did, to enact debauched fantasies in their individual silos, I kept an eye on what was *really* going on through the *Hōkūle'a*'s telescopes. And it was blindingly obvious that we were still in Earth orbit. That's how I realized this whole thing was a setup.

Conspiracy-minded? No, I just look at the facts. They must have known *someone* would realize we weren't going anywhere. That's why they didn't allow anyone except Letitia to communicate between the silos, do you see? I don't think it's a coincidence that the *Hōkūle'a* is shaped like a giant mushroom: they were keeping us in the dark and feeding us bullshit.

Yes, all right, that's a joke. But a big advantage of our clock being slowed down was that the real sky appeared sped up. In only an hour of subjective observing, five days passed outside. One could see the terminator crawling across the moon, easily witness the planets drifting against the background stars, and get dizzy watching Io whip around Jupiter.

And, God on high, the other things you can spot if you spend enough time doing astronomy! I made a whopping great discovery, you see, and—

Oh. You *do* know. Well, *fine.* Full marks. But it certainly left the great Captain Garvey gobsmacked when I told her!

Interview with Captain Letitia Garvey

In some ways, it would have been easier if I hadn't already downloaded. I could have used my unique ability as captain to pop my avatar from silo to silo, breaking the news to each member of my crew in turn. But, on the other hand, this way, only my voice would intrude on them. I'd been lucky when I'd forced my way into Jürgen's silo; he wasn't doing anything too decadent. God only knew what sorts of things the rest of my crew might have been up to.

I spoke into the workstation microphone. "Attention! Attention!" I waited ten seconds, repeated that, and then dove in, not sure exactly what I was going to say. "Hello, everyone. This is Letitia. I'm sure you're all expecting us to be arriving at Proxima Centauri b shortly. I've got bad news about that—and even worse news about Mother Earth. I'd tell you all to sit down—but there's no point in that, is there? Okay, here goes . . ."

And I told them.

I told them that our starship hadn't ever left Earth orbit.

I told them that their bodies were still in Waterloo.

And I told them that Waterloo was in ruins, and, I suspected, the rest of the planet was, too.

As I explained it all, thoughts that had been swirling in my mind started to coalesce. The reason our frozen bodies had never been loaded aboard the *Hōkūle'a* presumably was because civilization fell before that could happen.

Civilization fell.

Two words. Just like that. But, yes, surely it couldn't only be Waterloo that had been destroyed. I'd tried to make radio contact with Mission Control—which was in Darmstadt, Germany, part of the European Space Agency's contribution to our international project—and had gotten no response. In fact, as I'd told Jürgen, I'd failed to pick up any radio signals at all.

No plague could have ground civilization to a halt in the few days between when our bodies were frozen and when they should have been transferred to Mojave for shuttling up to our waiting starship. But whatever caused the catastrophe had spared both the *Hōkūleʻa*—whose telescopes I'd had no trouble accessing—and this building I was now in.

The *Hōkūleʻa:* built with heavy shielding for a mission to Proxima Centauri, a flare star with an enormously active magnetic field.

And the Quantum Cryonics Institute: constructed out of a series of interlocking Faraday cages designed to protect the delicate quantum computers it housed from electromagnetic interference.

It all fit.

It all made sense.

A coronal mass ejection.

The sun throwing off a giant wad of plasma, accompanied by a huge electromagnetic pulse. Such a thing had happened in the mid 1800s: the Carrington Event. It lit up skies as far south as Cuba with auroras bright enough to read by, fried telegraph wires, and even set telegraph paper on fire.

We'd been ripe for another such blast for a long time; it must have hit in November 2058, just after we'd uploaded. The accompanying EMP would have burned out electrical transformers all over the world, as well as wrecking huge numbers of computers and other electronic devices. All ten billion human beings would have been thrown into panic, starving in the dark.

There's only one good word for what it must have been like.

Doomsday.

Interview with Dr. Jürgen Haas

When I finally set Penolong down, the robot immediately turned around and scurried toward the operations center. But before he got halfway there he presumably realized it was too late to intervene and reversed course, rolling back to me.

"No," I said. "You were right the first time. Let's go see Letitia." But, as we discovered when we rounded a corner, she was already on her way to join us.

"*Qapla'*?" I asked.

"Yes," she said. "I have no idea how each of them took the news, but they certainly deserved to know." She shook her head. "Four years wasted."

I didn't think of them as wasted; they were, in fact, the best four years of my life so far—and given the devastation of the world outside, probably, I supposed, the best four years I would ever have.

Suddenly an alarm sounded. Penolong took off, treads spinning, toward the operations center. We ran behind him. The doors opened at Penolong's behest, and—

And my jaw dropped. The giant wall monitor was showing the interior of *another* cryonics chamber. The design of the cryo-coffins was different, and there were more of them. "What the hell?"

Letitia pointed at some smaller monitors. "And—God—it looks like *everyone* in that room is reviving."

"Can we abort it?"

"No. I mean, yes, there's an abort switch, but it's too dangerous. The bodies are already thawing out."

I looked at the image on the screen and quickly counted. Six rows of six beds: thirty-six corpsicles. Half again as many of them as of us. I turned to Penolong. "Do you know who these people are?"

"No," replied the robot. "That chamber is beyond my purview."

"Well, whoever they are, some of them might need help," said Letitia. "Penolong, do you at least know where that room is?"

"Yes." The robot raced out of the room and we sprinted behind him. He brought us to what looked like a bank-vault door. I tried pulling on the door's handle but it wouldn't budge.

"Can you open this?" Letitia asked.

"No," the robot replied. "That chamber is—"

"Is beyond your purview," I said. "Yeah, yeah. We know."

"But," said Penolong, "it's not beyond *her* purview." He pointed and I saw another robot, similar in boxy design to Penolong but not quite the same, coming toward us. As the gap between the two automatons closed, they began talking to each other the way sci-fi films had taught us robots should: in high-pitched squeals and bleeps. Actually, I think it was just English sped up to the maximum rate that the machines could parse. After a moment, the second robot must have sent a signal that unlocked the door because it swung open. Letitia and I hustled in, followed by both robots.

None of the cryobeds had opened yet, but the diagnostic display panels at the foot of each one showed the body temperatures rising rapidly. I did a quick jog up and down all six rows to see if any of the beds were damaged, but they all looked to be in fine shape.

The second robot was making the rounds of the beds, too, while Penolong parked himself in a corner.

The digital thermometers for each bed weren't quite in sync: some said thirty-one-point-something Celsius; some were in the thirty-twos and one had already passed thirty-three.

The unit to my left was the first to have its cover split down its length, with the halves sliding into pockets on either side, and—

Holy shit!

The damn body within arched upward as the built-in defibrillator jump-started its heart; my own, meanwhile, just about stopped when that happened. The body belonged to an Asian woman of about sixty. If all the bodies in here were elderly, then I guessed these were people who'd uploaded to try to cheat death.

Another capsule near me split open—it made me think of ribs being spread for heart surgery—and the body within, that of a white man, jumped as it, too, was defibrillated.

I remember *The Wrath of Khan*—an oldie but a goody—in which Spock transferred his entire *katra* into Dr. McCoy in a matter of seconds. I don't know how much information a *katra* contains, but a human consciousness is petabytes of data. Then again, these consciousnesses were being transferred instantaneously via quantum entanglement, so bandwidth constraints didn't apply. I watched as the eyes on the woman next to me fluttered open.

Letitia, over in the first row, was already helping a man there to his feet. He looked to be in his twenties—and so did a woman who was getting up on her own; so much for my theory that these people were mostly near the ends of their natural lifespans.

At the foot of the row I was in, another man—this one maybe thirty-five—was sitting up. He looked around but seemed to be having trouble focusing; maybe he normally wore glasses. After a second, his gaze landed on me. "Who the hell are you?" he demanded.

"Jürgen Haas. I'm a doctor."

"I don't need a goddamned doctor," he snapped. "I need a lawyer! Is that bitch Stella Rosen still in office? I demand to talk to her right now!"

I saw that Letitia was about to end up in a real altercation with the man she'd been trying to calm—and the rest of the people in the chamber were getting agitated, too. I don't like running away from confrontations, but thirty-six against two were odds only a fool would take. "Letitia," I said loudly, "scrub"—which was astronaut-speak for abort the mission.

For once our captain recognized the wisdom of my words. She made a beeline for the exit, followed by the two robots. I got there first, a head start being the only way I ever could beat Letitia in a race.

As soon as we were through the still-open heavy door, the second robot must have sent a signal again, and it began swinging shut. "The better part of valor," she quipped.

As the door was closing, a few of the recently defrosted decided to make a dash for it, but they were unsteady on their feet, and only the one who'd been yelling at me made it through in time. Once in the corridor, he leaned against the now-closed door and took a moment to catch his breath. Then he turned on Letitia. "Who are you?" he demanded.

"Letitia Garvey," she replied.

"And what the fuck do you do?"

"I'm an astronaut."

"The last fucking thing I need."

"And you?" said Letitia sharply. "Why were you in cryosleep?"

"I was serving time," he said.

"What?" I replied.

"Serving my sentence—which was up *years* ago."

"Sentence?" I said. "For what?"

"Murder." He gestured at the sealed chamber behind him. "Just like the most of the rest of them, I imagine."

I had the good sense not to say anything rash, and neither did Letitia. But little Penolong wasn't as circumspect. "Holy shit," he said.

CHAPTER 4

Interview with Captain Letitia Garvey

So there we were: face to face with a murderer. His name, I eventually learned, was Roscoe Koudoulian, and he'd tracked down and killed his childhood bully, something I could almost have sympathy for.

Roscoe was tall and muscular with brown hair graying at the temples. And he was seething—and I would be, too, if what he claimed was true: that his prison sentence should have ended four subjective years ago.

We were still just outside the closed vault door, Jürgen and me standing, while Roscoe—literally naked as a jaybird, a jailbird—was leaning against that door. Behind it were thirty-five other criminals, all, like him, with their consciousnesses re-integrated with their bodies just minutes ago. The two little robots were still with us: male-voiced Penolong and the female-voiced one whose name I'd yet to learn.

"What do you want to do now?" I asked Roscoe.

He indicated Jürgen with a thumb gesture. "Like I told this guy, see that bitch Stella Rosen."

"Who's that?" I asked.

"Head of the Massachusetts Department of Correction," he snapped. "Get her on video."

"I, ah, don't think she holds that office anymore." I found myself sidestepping the elephant in the—well, in the corridor.

"Then I want to go home," Roscoe said. "See my daughter Annabelle."

I looked at Jürgen. He lifted his hands slightly; it was his way of saying, "Do you tell him or should I?"

I turned back to the man. "I've got bad news, sir. There's been a disaster—maybe an EMP from a coronal mass ejection."

He looked at me as if I were speaking a foreign language. My first impulse was to explain all about the sun spitting out a giant chunk of plasma accompanied by a transformer-blowing electromagnetic pulse—not because I'm a natural teacher but because that was easier than telling him what the consequences of all that had been. But I simply cut to the chase. "It looks like most of the human race is dead."

Roscoe continued to stare at me for a few seconds then said, "What do you mean, 'Most of'? Don't you know?"

Jürgen replied: "We've only just downloaded, too."

"Then I *have* to go home," Roscoe said decisively. "Annabelle will need me."

"Where's home?" Jürgen asked.

"Buffalo, New York," said Roscoe.

It wasn't far—less than two hundred kilometers—but it would only be doable if he could find a working car and unbroken roads. I had no right to try to stop him . . . but there was a factor he wasn't taking into account. "Um, what year do you think this is?" I asked.

He scowled as if that were a stupid question. "Twenty sixty."

"No," I said. "No, it's not." I took a deep breath then exhaled. "It's 2548."

"Twenty-Five . . .?" He shook his head. "Bullshit," he said, but his tone was uncertain.

"It's true," confirmed Jürgen.

"I'm so sorry to say this," I said, gently, "but your daughter—she must be . . ."

Roscoe slumped further against the vault door, and the second robot rushed in to catch him, but the man managed to stay on his feet. Still, that robot reached up, took Roscoe's right hand, and led him over to a group of three chairs attached to the corridor wall. Roscoe lowered himself into the middle one, his bowed head moving slowly and ever so slightly from left to right, over and over again.

I crouched next to him and said "I'm sorry" once more. He slowly lifted his head and looked at me with red, watery eyes. "She was the whole point," he said softly. My puzzlement must have shown because after a moment he explained: "Annabelle was the reason I'd agreed to this cryonics shit."

Of course: it was the only way he could get out of prison in time to see her grow up. I'd gladly left behind everyone I'd ever known, except for my crew members, and there was no reason to think Roscoe's daughter hadn't lived a good, long life. Still, the sudden realization that he'd never see her again clearly was devastating. He looked at me a moment longer then lowered his head once more. I squeezed his shoulder and rose and walked back to Jürgen. The second robot rolled over to join us.

"What's your name?" I said to the machine.

"Wiidookaagewinini," the robot replied. "It's Anishinaabemowin for 'helper.' But you can just call me Wiidooka."

I tipped my head toward Roscoe but spoke to the robot. "Are all the people in there really like him? Convicts?"

"No, ma'am," said Wiidooka. I felt a knot that I hadn't realized was there loosening in my stomach. But Wiidooka went on: "Now, they're all *ex*-convicts. Their sentences have been served."

"Were they all the same length?"

"Yes. They were part of a pilot project, and so all should have been released the same day: 16 October 2060. During their sentences, the prison simulation was running at twenty-four times normal speed, so that date was ten objective months after their incarceration but twenty subjective years later for each of them. But when the release date rolled around, there were no humans left here to authorize their discharge, and so the clock governing their prison simulations automatically fell into line with the rest of the quantum computer—which was generating the simulations you and your fellow astronauts were in, running at just 1/120th of normal speed."

"So what caused the prisoners to be released now?" I asked.

Penolong, the male-voiced robot, had its robotic hands clasped behind its back in an at-ease posture, but its voice carried an I-told-you-so tone. "I suspect when you adjusted the overall clock speed of the quantum computer, a failsafe was tripped and automatic downloading began."

"Speaking of which," said Wiidooka, "I can't leave them locked up in there. For one thing, they'll get hungry soon."

As soon as the robot said that, I realized I was famished myself—a sensation I hadn't experienced in years. "Is there any food?"

"Oh, yes," said Wiidooka. "The cafeteria in the basement is up and running now."

I didn't understand how that could possibly be the case, but one doesn't look a gift robot in the speaker grille. "Let's get something to eat," I said to Jürgen. And then, although I wasn't really sure I wanted to make the offer, I added, "Sir, do you care to join us?"

He'd been sitting with his head in his hands, and when he looked up his expression was one of bewilderment and loss. "What?"

"Care for some food?" I said.

He shook his head.

Wiidooka was turning to face the door between us and the criminals. "Wait!" I said. "At least give us a head start. I'm not ready to deal with thirty-five other pissed-off prisoners."

The robot considered. "They are no longer prisoners . . . but I suppose after all this time, another half hour won't hurt."

"If any of them need medical help," said Jürgen, "come get me."

Wiidooka nodded its brick-shaped head. There was a brief interchange of super-high-speed English between the two robots, then Penolong said at normal speed, "Please come with me; I'll take you to the cafeteria."

I nodded but spoke to Wiidooka. "Will you explain to them what's happened?"

"Yes," the robot replied, and then, rather wistfully, it added, "I just hope they don't take their anger out on me."

Interview with Roscoe Koudoulian

Wiidooka opened the vault door, and I listened from the entrance as she told my fellow prisoners what the hell was going on. They shouted questions at her while getting dressed; whatever clothes they'd brought to prison were still in their vacuum-sealed footlockers here. After they ran out of questions—and invective—the little robot said the words we'd waited so many years to hear: "You're free to go." Ex-cons started pouring out of the chamber like . . . well, like that horrific sight I'd had to relive over and over again: blood gushing from Mitch Aldershot's chest.

There were nineteen other men and sixteen women. I didn't recognize any of them, of course. The people I'd thought of as my fellow inmates had all been simulations— and not a one of these actual flesh-and-blood humans smiled at me as they passed.

I went in, found my footlocker, and got dressed. Seems I was the only one who'd brought a suit and tie to prison; the rest were now wearing hoodies or T-shirts.

I was all alone, and I savored that for a time—funny, after being in what had actually been solitary for almost a quarter of a century. But, no, that wasn't right. It probably now really was all those hundreds of years later, and, even if this disaster, whatever the hell it was, hadn't happened, my beloved Annabelle would have been long dead from—Jesus, what a thought!—from old age.

There was part of me that wanted to scramble back into my hibernation unit, its top gaping open in front of me like a pair of jaws. At least in there, in my virtual world, I could keep watching the videos of Annabelle at school, at the playground, having fun, being *alive*.

What had she been like, I wondered, as a teenager? As a wife, a mother—God, maybe even a grandmother? I hope she'd experienced all of that. I used to tell her, back when she was a toddler and I was bouncing her on my knee, that someday all her dreams might come true. I hoped more than anything that they had.

I don't know how long I just stood there, contemplating my daughter's fate, but I eventually became aware of my stomach growling. The robot with the male voice had said the cafeteria was in the basement, and I set off to find it.

Along the way, I came upon a large window and got my first glimpse of the outside world: trees erupting through broken asphalt and mangled sidewalks; tall grasses and weeds filling the cracks; buildings slumped down, looking as defeated as I felt.

When I got to the cafeteria, I found most of my fellow prisoners had also come down there. Some were seated in small groups; others were eating alone. Wiidooka caught sight of me, rolled over, and led me inside. "Where does the food come from?" I asked.

"The institute had a staff of more than four hundred. When civilization fell, we froze all the food in this building. We keep bodies frozen here for centuries; foodstuffs were a piece of cake—speaking of which, would you like one?"

"No. But maybe some beef?"

"Ah," said Wiidooka, and she sounded disapproving. "Not a vegan. Well, let's see what we can find."

She located a plastic bag of beef stew, which she heated in a microwave. I took my tray over to a table that had five people at it. "Mind if I join you?" I asked.

Two of the five completely ignored me. Another grunted. But an obese white guy in a white T-shirt with hair that looked like it was meant to be slicked back but now hung in bangs said, "Why not?"

I sat down. "My name's Roscoe."

The fat guy snorted. "First Roscoe I ever met."

"And you are?" I asked.

"Alan," he said. "Alan Smithee."

It was my turn to snort. For many years, Alan Smithee was the only pseudonym the Directors Guild of America allowed members to use; some of the greatest stinkers in movie history were directed by Alan Smithee. But if this guy didn't care to give his real name, that was fine by me. Maybe he was a famous murderer—someone whose name I'd have recognized—and he didn't want his past following him into this new existence.

As I ate my stew, I looked around. There were cracks in the ceiling and stains on the walls from where water had trickled down, although they stopped a meter and a half above the floor. Ah: that must have been the highest the robots could reach to do repairs.

I supposed we could stay in this building indefinitely—although the only beds were probably the hard slabs in the cryo-coffins. But I didn't want to do that, and I hoped some of the others wouldn't, either. Still, making our way in a ruined city didn't sound easy. Alan looked like a tough customer, and several of the others appeared rough-and-tumble, too. But it would take more than brute strength to live out there. It'd take survival skills.

And who has survival training?

Astronauts, that's who.

Letitia and . . . what was his name? Jürgen, that's it. Letitia and Jürgen. They'd know—hell, they'd know how to start a fire and skin a deer. And wasn't Jürgen a doctor? He'd know how to set a broken bone or suture up a wound. I stood. As I pushed my chair back, it made a chalk-on-blackboard sound . . . something I'd only ever heard in movies; smartboards just didn't make that screech.

"Where you going?" Alan Smithee asked.

"To see some astronauts."

"*Fine,*" he snarled. "*Don't* tell me."

Interview with Dr. Jürgen Haas

There had been no need to eat back in my virtual heaven, but food was a sensual pleasure, and I'd often conjured up my favorite dishes. There's nothing like a rare porterhouse—and a guilt-free imaginary one, at that—with its juices running onto the plate, accompanied by asparagus spears in béarnaise sauce and a steaming baked potato with all the fixings.

God only knows if I'll ever get to enjoy a virtual or actual meal like that again. Still, the chow from the institute cafeteria that Letitia and I wolfed down made freeze-dried astronaut rations seem like the best Barberian's Steak House had to offer by comparison. But we wanted to clear out before the pack of criminals arrived.

As soon as we were done, we headed up from the basement and took our first steps outside. It was hot—over thirty degrees, I estimated—which was crazy for Waterloo in February. I had hoped, given civilization had apparently fallen five hundred years ago, that global warming would have reversed, but apparently it hadn't.

The concrete slabs in front of the entrance were broken, and giant sinkholes had opened in the roadways. The trees, shrubs, and weeds that pushed up through every fissure were all lushly green, and water was pooling in various declivities.

We hiked for a couple of hours, getting the lay of the land. Near what was left of University Avenue, we saw a half-dozen deer nipping at vegetation. They eyed us without fear as we passed. Beautiful animals, but the sight of them made me sad. My younger brother had died from cancer when I was thirty, and he'd had his condo filled with photos and paintings of deer.

Letitia was ready to go farther, but I held up a hand and lowered myself onto a concrete bench covered by lichen. It was in the shade of an office building. "My God," I said, my breathing labored. "I haven't been . . . been *tired* for years!"

Letitia sat next to me and used the sleeve of her jumpsuit to wipe sweat from her brow. "Copy that, big guy," she said, "I was ready to leave everyone I'd ever met behind. Family, friends, neighbors, all of them: buh-bye. But I'd always thought, even after we made it to Proxima Centauri, that when I looked up at the night sky, when I saw our sun adding an extra jag to Cassiopeia, that there'd still be humans there—humans *here*—thriving, inventing, doing things."

I shook my head. "I knew it'd end like this. When I was a kid, we worried about climate change and a nuclear holocaust and biological or cyber warfare and an artificial-intelligence uprising. Some sort of human-caused catastrophe. But that's never been the threat. Mother Nature just fucking hates us. Earthquakes and hurricanes and plagues like COVID-19 and COVID-50, plus a whopping great solar coronal mass ejection, for fuck's sake. She just wants us *gone*."

"Well," Letitia said, "maybe you're right; maybe Mother Nature didn't like what she gave birth to *here*. Tell the truth, I didn't much like it, either." She paused, and I expected her to say something about man's inhumanity to man, but no, what I got was classic Letitia. "So much fucking incompetence," she said, shaking her head. "So many asswipes here who couldn't do anything right." She waved vaguely at the sky. "But up there? There has to be something better than the people we were going to leave behind—has to be."

I made a noncommittal grunt and slowly swung my gaze around, taking in the ruins. She did the same thing. In places, forest had completely reclaimed the land; in other spots, such as where we were sitting, heaps of bricks or the twisted skeletons of buildings bore silent witness to the thriving metropolis that had once been here. I let out a long, whispery sigh. "What a mess."

She gestured at the sky again. "The *Hōkūleʻa* is up there, in orbit. If we could just get to it, we could still head for Proxima."

I snorted. "Even if there's some survivor encampment somewhere, they almost certainly don't have space shuttles."

"Have you got a better idea?" she snapped.

"Sure. We could re-upload."

"Crawl back into your hole, you mean?"

"Why not? There's nothing for us here. We could spend eternity, each of us happy in our individual—"

"Bespoke heavens?" Letitia's voice was thick with sarcasm. "The point of the whole damn exercise—the reason the Alliance of National Space Agencies spent a trillion dollars building a starship—was to get a nucleus of humans established a safe distance away. You mentioned COVID-50: there is—there *was*—enough travel between Earth and the Mars colony that a plague could easily wipe out both populations. Our job—yours, mine, and the other twenty-two of us—was to make sure *Homo sapiens,* crappy species though it might be, survived. Well, we *have* survived, but we didn't do it so you could spend eternity jacking off in some solipsistic fantasy land."

I folded my arms in front of my chest. "So, what are you going to do? Force the others to download?"

"We need all hands on deck. Scouting parties; engineering teams. Once we find a way to reach our starship, we can all go back into hibernation—and head off to where we're meant to be."

"It's pointless," I said. "It's a five-hundred-year journey to Proxima Centauri. We're lucky the quantum computer has lasted *this* long; no complex machine humans have ever built has functioned for a full millennium."

There was a desperation in Letitia's voice I'd never heard before. "It *will* continue to work. It has to."

"Now who's living in a fantasy land?" I snapped. "Leave the rest of the crew where they are. Let them enjoy their lives."

"That's not living."

"Says the fearless leader."

"Don't be an ass, Jürgen. We have to—"

But whatever additional craziness she was going to spout was cut off by a loud, piercing scream.

Interview with Captain Letitia Garvey

Yes, sure, I was pissed at Jürgen—*this* Jürgen. The man I'd known before we'd uploaded would have been right by my side, fighting for even the slimmest chance to save our mission. We were supposed to never give up, to never surrender. But he *had* surrendered, seduced by unreality.

And yet when we heard that scream, he was on his feet before I was, running toward its source. His body was still reviving: he was unsteady as he picked up speed. I followed and found myself wobbly, too, as I jumped across potholes and scrabbled over tree trunks.

Soon, there was another scream, this one muffled. I had trouble fixing where it came from, but Jürgen headed to our left. There was a low brick wall next to us, part of the remains of some long-collapsed building. We ran along its length, rounding the end simultaneously.

The remnants of another wall ran parallel to it six or seven meters away, and a large white man had pushed a white teenaged girl against the red bricks. The girl was wearing a simple black dress that looked handmade, and the man—

—the man had creepy bloodshot eyes and was wearing twenty-first-century clothes: tennis shoes, blue jeans, a T-shirt with the name of a rock band on it. He must have been one of the prisoners. He'd pulled his jeans down to mid-thigh, exposing his ass to us—meaning his penis was grinding against the girl, who was trying to push him off. He was struggling to get her long dress hiked up enough to enter her.

Jürgen was on him in a flash, grabbing his shoulder from behind and spinning him around. The motion clearly left them both unsure of their footing—but, since the other guy was presumably one of the defrosted prisoners, at least Jürgen had the advantage of having been reanimated a few hours longer. He recovered his balance more quickly.

As soon as there was a gap between her and her attacker, the girl slid to the side and escaped. The asshole was bigger than Jürgen, but not in as good shape, and Jürgen hit him with a right cross that knocked him against the bricks.

"The fuck, man?" shouted the guy.

Jürgen was livid. "This is what you do as soon as you get out? *This?*"

The girl was running away as fast as she could. I didn't blame her; I'd have done the same thing. But I had to know who she was and what other people were still alive, so I took off after her. She was nimble as a mountain goat as she hurried across the twisted landscape, but her long black dress wasn't made for running and she soon came up against the ruins of another wall, preventing her going any farther. I was still unsteady but had no trouble catching up to her.

She was sixteen or seventeen and clearly terrified. But, as she looked at me, her eyes were wide, as if in astonishment. I smiled my most reassuring smile and asked, "Are you all right?," but she didn't reply. She was trembling, still terrified, and I guess I instinctively opened my arms to embrace her. She hesitated for a moment, then collapsed against me, sobbing. I held her, gently stroking her blond hair and making soothing sounds. After a little while, Jürgen joined us. I looked over the girl's shoulder at him. "What happened to that asshole?"

"I let him go," Jürgen said, but before I could protest, he went on. "There are no cops to call, right? No jail to haul him off to. And nothing to hog-tie the son of a bitch with. But, after I threatened to snap his arm off, I *did* get his name. Hornbeck. He was one of the prisoners. I told him if he touches this girl, or anyone else, ever again, I'd break his fucking neck."

The girl moved in a way that suggested she wanted me to let go of her, and I did. She looked at Jürgen. *"Tonk yo,"* she said. *"Tonk yo. Tonk yo."*

It was gibberish to me, but Jürgen got it. "She's saying 'thank you.'"

"So you speak English?" I said to her.

She frowned.

Jürgen tried, *"Sprechen Sie Deutsch?"* But that got no response, either.

"Where do you suppose she's from?" I asked.

It was Jürgen's turn to frown—but then his eyebrows shot up as if he'd had an epiphany. "From right around here," he said. That seemed a pointlessly obvious observation, but he went on. "Look at how she's dressed."

She was still shaking, but her head was tilted to one side, clearly baffled by our strange language. Her clothes, as I'd noted before, were simple and all black, and, despite the heat, quite concealing. "Yes?" I said, irritated.

"I bet she was wearing a bonnet that got lost in the attack," he added.

"For Christ's sake, just tell me."

He seemed disappointed that I hadn't gotten it. "She's a Mennonite."

Jürgen was from nearby Toronto, but I'd only spent a few weeks here in Waterloo while we were preparing to upload my crew, and I'd never had time to venture into the surrounding communities. But, yes, I had occasionally seen black-clad folk making their way slowly down the side roads in horse-drawn buggies.

And, when I'd arrived, I'd read a brief history of this area. The high-tech industry that had grown up around here had started with the company that invented the first smartphone, the BlackBerry. The co-founder of that company, Mike Lazaridis, had once been asked whether he considered it ironic that his firm was surrounded by people who would never use its products. His response? "I love the Mennonites. They're the backup plan for humanity."

And so, it seemed, they were. Not us. Not astronauts, not engineers, not those who depended on electrical grids, computers, microchips, and other advanced technology.

And this violated and frightened girl in front of us was living, breathing proof that the backup plan had worked.

Interview with Dr. Jürgen Haas

The Mennonite girl's name, we managed to figure out, was Sarah. Although she was speaking a form of English, Letitia and I found it very hard to understand. Well, it *had* been five hundred years, and languages and their pronunciations drift, all the more so, I imagine, when you have no TV, movies, radio, or audiobooks to lock in a standard way of speaking.

We managed to convey to Sarah that we'd like to meet her again tomorrow. Although the simplest notion to get across would have been for us to rendezvous where we'd first encountered her, Letitia pointed out that no one wants to return to where they were almost raped. Sarah walked with us for as long as her path home apparently coincided with ours. When we parted, about half an hour after the sun had set, we agreed to meet at that spot, at midday tomorrow—at least, I hoped she understood that that was when we'd be back; I'd pointed at the last glow of sunlight on the horizon, then made a sweeping arc with my arm from east to west, to indicate the sun's track across the sky, and then did it again, stopping halfway and pointing up emphatically. After a few repetitions, she seemed to get it.

Letitia and I were then only a kilometer from the institute, but it took us over an hour to pick our way through the brush and rubble. Unlike in my virtual silo, there was no full moon—or any moon—to illuminate the landscape. But lights were on in the various windows of the institute, and they helped guide us to it.

As we got closer, I heard a desperate male voice: "Dr. Haas! Captain Garvey!"

It was difficult to see, but at last I made out the sight of poor Penolong. The silly robot had ventured onto the broken pavement in front of the institute and had tipped partway into a fissure his treads couldn't get him out of.

"What are you doing out here?" I said as we closed the distance to him.

The robot sounded anxious. "I've been trying to find you. Some of the prisoners are attempting to break into the quantum-computing chamber."

"*Oh, shit!*" Letitia exclaimed as she started running.

I picked up Penolong, who seemed a lot heavier after a day of hiking than he had before, and we hustled back into the institute. I don't think anyone had anticipated an attack on the great tetrahedral quantum computer, but its chamber was heavily insulated in hopes of preventing decoherence. When we made it to the second floor, we saw four men and three women using a conference table as a battering ram to try to break through the chamber's sealed metal door. It looked like it would give way any minute now.

"What the hell are you doing?" I shouted.

They paused. "Who are you?" demanded a broad-shouldered white guy.

"Jürgen Haas. I'm a doctor."

"You ever hear of a prison break, doc?" said the same man. "Well, we're gonna break this prison." He snickered, delighted at his own wit. "No fucking way they can lock us in there again and forget about us for centuries."

"We've still got people in there," Letitia said imploringly. "They'll die if you perturb the quantum computer."

The man's voice was pure ice. "I've killed before." And he and his cronies went back to smashing the table against the buckling door.

Letitia turned and ran toward the operations center in the next room. Penolong and I followed as fast as we could. "What are you doing?" I asked her as we entered.

"I'm going to download everyone," she said, lowering herself into a chair in front of the blue-green hockey-puck computer she'd used before.

And, in that moment, I realized our earlier argument was moot. As much as virtual existence had represented heaven for us astronauts, it had been hell for the prisoners—and there was no way the two of us could protect the quantum computer from an angry, violent mob. What Letitia was about to do was the only chance of survival for the rest of our crew.

"Login," she said. "Letitia Garvey."

"Hello, Letitia," replied the puck. "What can I do for you?"

"Initiate downloading of the *Hōkūleʻa* astronauts," she commanded over top of the pounding of the makeshift battering ram. "And, for the love of God, hurry!"

CHAPTER 5

Interview with Captain Letitia Garvey

As soon as the computer acknowledged that the downloading of my starship crew had begun, Jürgen, Penolong, and I hustled over to the astronaut cryonics chamber. Of course, my cryo-coffin was open, and so was Jürgen's, and—

—and *shit!* In all the commotion, I'd forgotten about Mikhail Sidorov, our ship's roboticist. *His* open coffin really *was* a coffin, with his desiccated corpse and its smashed-in skull lying inside. There was no way any consciousness could download into *that.*

Jürgen was a physician; he was needed here as defibrillators were going off like popcorn popping. But I could be spared. I ran back into the corridor, hoping to talk the seven prisoners who were trying to bash in the door to the quantum-computing chamber into stopping. But, just as I arrived, they succeeded in knocking it down. The three female ex-cons and the four male ones burst into the room that held the giant computer.

I followed them in. "Please!" I called out. "Please don't. There's a man trapped inside!"

The same surly guy who'd confronted us before looked at me. "Against his will?" he sneered. "Unable to get out even though his time is up? Cry me a fucking river."

Although their minds had each spent twenty-four subjective years inside it, I suspected none of them had ever laid eyes on this, or any, quantum computer before. The other three men were walking around the tetrahedron's base, which measured fifteen meters on a side, presumably looking for some external component they could easily wreck. Meanwhile, a thick-bodied woman had taken a fire extinguisher off its wall mount and was slamming the heavy tank against one of the computer's mirrored triangular faces.

I was about to yell "Stop!" when, by a split second, another voice—a male one—beat me to it. I pivoted, and there was Roscoe Koudoulian, accompanied by six other people who I presumed were also recently downloaded prisoners. "You heard the lady," he said. "There's at least one person left in there."

"Who cares?" sneered the same man, whose name, I discovered later, was Caleb.

The guy immediately behind Roscoe was enormous, maybe a hundred and fifty kilos; I eventually learned that he went by the name Alan Smithee. "*I* care," he growled. "The only intact technology for miles around is right here in this building. Who knows what we're going to need to survive?"

The woman with the fire extinguisher had made a sizable dent in the triangular side of the computer, but she hadn't ruptured its housing yet. The banging of metal against metal was echoing loudly in the chamber.

Caleb was defiant. "We're not going to need this fucking thing."

"Maybe not," said Roscoe. "But you might need a doctor at some point." He indicated me. "Her friend Jürgen is one."

I nodded emphatically. "And we have another MD downloading right now."

"So," said Roscoe, "it's better not to piss them off."

"Get the hell out," Caleb sneered at Roscoe, "or it's you who'll need a doctor."

Alan Smithee lumbered forward. "You think you can take me?"

Caleb was the same height as Alan Smithee but probably only massed half as much. Still, he looked like he was seriously considering taking a swing at Alan. For his part, Alan made beckoning come-and-get-it gestures with both hands.

The three men had finished circumnavigating the quantum computer's base; they appeared ready to give Caleb backup. Meanwhile, the others who had come with Roscoe fanned out behind Smithee.

I didn't want a brawl, especially between people who had murdered before, but at least this was buying time—maybe not enough to save Mikhail, but precious seconds that might still be needed to complete the downloading of my crew.

The woman who'd been pounding on the reflective side of the computer's shell was still at it, and—

—and there's a reason a quantum-computing center and a facility for cryogenically freezing human bodies were housed in the same building. Both depended on supercooling materials, the former to minimize atomic vibrations so qubits don't accidentally flip quantum states, the latter to preserve body tissues against decay.

When I first saw the white cloud, I thought the woman's fire extinguisher had gone off, but, no, that wasn't it. Rather, she'd succeeded in putting a crack in one side of the computer's housing, and liquid nitrogen, at almost two hundred degrees below zero, came shooting out in a geyser. The woman staggered backward—and slipped on what was now an icy floor. The stream of nitrogen fire-hosed onto her face.

Meanwhile, one of the three men behind Caleb dropped like a sack of potatoes. I knew what was happening, but I doubt they did: liquid nitrogen has an expansion ratio of almost seven hundred to one; a single liter of it boils off to seven hundred liters of nitrogen gas, and that displaces the oxygen in any confined space.

"Get out!" I shouted even as I started running for the exit. "Get out!"

Roscoe and Alan were hot on my heels, but I saw Caleb fall unconscious to the floor. It turned out to be a good thing that the mob had knocked the large door to the chamber completely off its hinges. White clouds were billowing out into the corridor, and I suspected enough breathable air was moving back into the chamber that no one who'd fallen would asphyxiate to death. Still, as soon as I felt it was safe, Roscoe, Alan Smithee, and I went back in and pulled Caleb and the other man, both of whom were still unconscious, to safety.

But the woman who had caused this mess was dead, dead, dead. She hadn't shattered like a goldfish dropped in liquid nitrogen, but her body was as frozen as any of ours had been during hibernation—and without the benefit of her bodily water and blood first being replaced by antifreeze. Throughout her body and brain, cells must have burst wide open as they froze.

We'd been revived for less than a day now, and we'd already had our first death, not to mention our first mob violence, plus the attempted rape of Sarah, the Mennonite girl. It was a pretty poor start to our lives in this, our brave new twenty-sixth-century world.

Interview with Valentina Solomon

No, *don't* call me that. My name is Valentina. It's in honor of Valentina Tereshkova, the first woman in space. And, no, of course I wasn't going to be the first woman to Proxima Centauri; half the *Hōkūle'a*'s crew is female. But I *would* have been the first person like me to travel to another star—if, that is, our so-called starship had ever gotten underway.

Four years is a long time to spend . . . well, to spend with *yourself.* You learn a lot about who you are. And you've got the power, in your personal silo, to shape reality any way you wish.

Sure, we were all leaving our families behind. In my case, that meant my mother, my father, and my brother. But I admit I re-created them—or at least versions of them—in my virtual world. It's intoxicating, editing the characteristics of other people. My mom's judgmentalism? Gone. My father's prejudice? Out the window. Even my brother, who is—who *was*—pretty cool, got his frenetic energy taken down a notch, not to mention his booming voice. Noah—that was his name—always spoke too loudly, as if he were on some imaginary stage playing to the back row. Well, on *my* imaginary stage, he talked like a normal person.

And, in my silo, my family was exactly as supportive as I wanted them to be. All in all, I was pretty happy in there. I hear some of my crewmates went for wild existences during the time we thought we were *en route* to Proxima b—endless orgies, apparently, and bloody gladiatorial combat, too, and they say Per Lindstrom started his own religion and spent most of those four years being worshipped by parishioners he'd conjured up. But me, I just wanted peace and quiet, you know? No *tsuris,* as my *bubbe* would say. Just acceptance.

So you can imagine how I felt when I was ripped without warning from all of that.

I'd been playing chess. I'm a good chess player—not great, but good—and I'd conjured up an opponent who had exactly my skill level. He was playing white and had just taken one of my bishops. I was irritated but thought I could get his queen in three moves. And then, suddenly, I felt a tingling all over and my vision flashed between negative and positive images: the black chess pieces becoming white, and vice versa, maybe three times a second. My first thought was that I was having a stroke, but I *couldn't* be; I was an uploaded consciousness, not a physical brain, and there were no blood vessels to rupture.

My vision stabilized and I saw that my simulated opponent looked as shocked as I felt. His mouth was hanging open and his eyebrows had gone way up. I had no idea what he was seeing as he stared at me, nor did I yet have any idea what was happening.

And then the world around me—the world I'd made, the world I felt safe in—fragmented into tiny pieces, pixels of unreality, and suddenly I found myself back in the physical realm, inside—

They call it a cryo-coffin out of a kind of bravado, I suppose, but it really did feel like a coffin just then. It wasn't as though I was coming back to life; it was like I was dying.

My heart was already beating at this point, and I felt cold. My head pounded, my mouth was parched, and my skin itched—sensations I hadn't had even once in the last four years. And . . .

And *damn.*

Damn, damn, damn, damn, damn.

I was naked, of course, and as I pushed the thermal blanket off and tipped my head down, I took in the sight of the body I'd woken up in. The flat, hairy chest; the muscular arms, also hairy; and, between my legs, shriveled from the cold, a penis.

I sat up in the coffin, like Dracula come dusk, and took in the scene. I wasn't the only one being yanked back to reality. All the other coffins were open, too. Some of their occupants had already hauled themselves to their feet and were getting dressed. Others were still sitting or lying down.

Dr. Haas was making his rounds, checking on each of the newly awoken. He looked steady on his feet, so I assumed he'd downloaded a while ago. As he passed my coffin, he said, "You okay?" I nodded, removing the leads plugged into this body, and he continued on to the next person.

But I was far, far from okay. I was furious. How dare they pull me back from my heaven? How fucking dare they?

The whole room was freezing, I suppose as a result of all those cryochambers splitting open at once; I desperately wanted to put on clothes. I managed to clamber out of the coffin and, holding onto it for support with one hand, I worked my way to the footlocker. There was a loud pop as I broke the vacuum seal. My olive-green astronaut jump suit was in there, neatly folded. I shimmied into it, looked down, and—

The *Hōkūleʻa* wasn't a military vessel; it was a purely civilian one, and so our jumpsuits didn't have our last names on them. I'd once joked that we looked like garage mechanics, because our fabric nameplates instead gave first names. But I wasn't laughing now. There, over my lack of a left breast, was the one I hated, the one I loathed, the one I'd never wanted to hear again.

I dug my short fingernails under the edge of the fabric and spent the next ten minutes tearing the nameplate off. Like I said, my name is Valentina now, even if I'm stuck in this goddamned male body, and I'll thank you to never, ever deadname me again.

Interview with Dr. Jürgen Haas

I slept like a sack of shit that first night. All but one of the two dozen members of the *Hōkūleʻa*'s crew were now revived, the exception being our expert in robotics, Mikhail Sidorov, whose mind was still stuck inside the quantum computer with no place to go. And the thirty-five surviving prisoners were out raising havoc, too.

Besides the attack on the computer, those thugs managed several fistfights among themselves, and there were a few punch-ups between some of them and a couple of our pricklier astronauts. Of course, the institute had an infirmary, and, although the pharmaceuticals and anesthetics there had expired centuries ago, I was pleased to see that some of the supplies were still intact. I stitched up one prisoner's face, and I made a splint for Per Lindstrom, who I guess didn't find the ex-cons as pliant as his made-up worshipers. But at least for the time being, the eruption of liquid nitrogen had cooled the convicts on the idea of further smashing up the quantum computer. Ha! See what I did there? "Cooled them." Thank you, thank you, I'm here all millennium.

Anyway, although the rest of our crew had just awoken, Letitia and I had been up for hours and were both frankly exhausted. The cryo-coffins were no good for sleeping; they had no padding. Letitia found a musty couch, most of its stuffing decayed to dust, in the office of the institute's director, and I made a little bed in another office out of a row of chairs. But sleep didn't come easily; I kept thinking one of those damn prison-types was going to slip a shiv between my ribs. Fortunately, Jameela Chowdhury, our British astrophysicist, agreed to stand watch for a few hours, and then someone else would relieve her.

The next morning, as planned, Letitia and I headed out to rendezvous with Sarah, the Mennonite teenager. Our convict buddy Roscoe wanted to come along. He'd read up on Mennonites and many other societies while in prison and said he wanted to see what Sarah's community looked like. Well, why not?

It was another scorchingly hot day; I never thought I'd miss old-style Canadian winters! But at last we reached the point where we'd parted from Sarah yesterday. She was sitting on some rubble, just staring into space. It wasn't so much her clothes—a demure light gray dress today, with a white bonnet—that struck me as strange. Rather, I couldn't remember the last time I'd seen someone killing time who wasn't doing something on their phone.

As we approached, a big man emerged from behind some trees; I think he'd been taking a leak. He was dressed in rustic black pants and a simple off-white shirt and had a full blond beard.

Sarah introduced him as her "brutter," and said his name was Joshua. Of course: she hadn't wanted to come meet us on her own, knowing Hornbeck was out there somewhere. I introduced Roscoe as our friend.

We all headed off toward their home. Sarah and Joshua leapt easily from one pile of rubble to the next. Letitia, Roscoe, and I had trouble keeping up.

We'd hiked for about an hour, the sun beating down from a cloudless blue sky, when Letitia suddenly came to a stop. I guess Sarah previously had no reason to be on the lookout for people following her, and Roscoe, Joshua, and I were utterly oblivious, but Letitia had lived that wary existence of a woman on pre-disaster Earth. Something alerted her, and, as she swung around, I saw him, too: Hornbeck, the same prisoner who had attacked Sarah yesterday. He quickly lowered himself behind a pile of glacial erratics, but my guess was that he'd figured where there was one pretty young woman to attack there was bound to be another and another. Sarah hadn't spotted him before he hid, which I suppose was a good thing; if she had, she might have run off, never to be seen again.

But I wasn't going to let the motherfucker get away. I ran in his direction, and Roscoe and Letitia followed. The bastard must have heard me coming because he popped up again from behind the rocks and took off. Roscoe blocked his only escape route, and I slammed Hornbeck to the ground—for the second time in twenty-four hours.

He looked terrified, and well he should have. I was ready to do to him what had been done to Mikhail Sidorov—smash his skull in. "Are you out of your mind?" I shouted into Hornbeck's face. "Soon as I get my hands on a scalpel, I'm going to castrate you."

He spit at me, getting gob on my chin. And that was *it.* I started whaling on the asshole with both fists. Yeah, I'd left her behind five hundred years ago, but my sister had been raped once—I've got no use for human garbage who does that.

"Who are you?" demanded Hornbeck. "The fucking police?" I kept pounding and pounding. Blood poured out of his nostrils and the sides of his mouth.

It was Roscoe—yeah, Roscoe Koudoulian, the convicted murderer—who finally pulled me off the guy. I fought against his grip for a bit, but he was right; this was no way to deal with Hornbeck. As I caught my breath, I turned around and saw Sarah and Joshua, the pacifist Mennonites, standing there with their mouths hanging open in absolute horror.

Interview with Sarah Good

Dear God, this is hard. No, no, I'll be all right, but . . . just *thinking* about what happened to me is so upsetting.

And—my goodness! You've done something to my voice, haven't you? Making my English sound like Jürgen's. Well, okay, I guess, but please do put it back to normal when we're done.

Honestly, though, I don't even know if I should be talking to you. No, it's not because you're an outsider, even though that name hasn't really meant anything for a long time now. It's because you're not really *here.* I can see you, and you look real, but I've—God, that was terrifying! My hand passed right through you!

I've never heard that term before. "Hollow gram?"

Oh, yes, naturally, I've seen myself in pools of water. You're saying you're like that, a reflection? Hmmm. I guess.

Forgive me, but you look *so* odd. I thought it was weird that Letitia's skin is brown—but yours is blue! And, my goodness, your height! None of this makes sense to me.

You want to know about my community? Well, we're Mennonites. Deacon says, way in the past, we were called "Old Order" Mennonites, or "horse-and-buggy" Mennonites, because there were others who claimed they belonged to the same faith but used fancy machines and such. But all those other Mennonites are gone, along with everyone else—well, everyone except those like Jürgen from the past who are with us now. And, no, I don't understand any of that, either!

We have a good-sized community. Farmers, mostly, like my father, but some craftsmen, too. My brother Joshua is a blacksmith. Me, I'm a scavenger. Others say I'm good at finding useful things in the ruins, including scrap metal for Joshua to work with. That's what I was doing the day that . . . that awful . . .

I'm sorry. I don't mean to cry. Just—just give me a moment, please. It was *such* a shock. We Mennonites, we're a peace-loving people. That's what Christ taught, and that's the way we live. To . . . to attack someone the way I was! I—I have nightmares about it. I've had to fend off dogs and wolves while scavenging, but another *person?* It was *horrible.* I knew he wasn't one of us by how he was dressed. I'd never seen an outsider before him, and I'll be thankful if I never see another one again.

No, you're right. It *was* other outsiders who saved me. Letitia and Jürgen. Decent folk, both of them. Although, the next day, the way Jürgen *beat* the man who . . . who attacked me. I've never seen such . . . such . . .

Yes, "savagery" *is* a good word for it. I was grateful to him—I mean, he did save me! But I also hated what he did. It's not our way. Christ said, "You've heard the saying, 'an eye for an eye and a tooth for a tooth.' But I'm telling you, don't resist evil people. If somebody slaps you on the right cheek, offer him your left one, too." But what that man tried to do to me wasn't just a slap. It was . . . it was *monstrous*. He—he tried to . . . he wanted to . . .

I'm sorry. Just . . . just . . . it's just so awful.

What? Oh. That *is* a good question. I'll have to ask the bishop. Me, I have no idea what should be done with violent people. I'd never met one before. I didn't think they *existed* anymore.

Really? Your people don't have any violence, either? That's good to hear—very good, indeed. At least we have that much in common!

Interview with Roscoe Koudoulian

Yes, yes, I've admitted it: I killed a man. Fucking Mitch Aldershot, my childhood tormentor. But you're asking if I'd kill Aldershot again if I had it to do over?

I had twenty-four years to think about that while in virtual prison, and, as I said, they made me relive the crime again and again from various perspectives. By the way, I was a model prisoner—I should have been paroled early, if anything—so thanks fucking heaps for the extra four years at the end of my sentence. No, no, I know it's not your fault, but it still pisses me off. Not as much as it infuriates Caleb or some of the others, but it sure as shit wasn't fair.

Anyway, no, I would not have killed Aldershot if I had a do-over. Dude was *nasty,* y'know, but he didn't deserve to die. And, yes, sure, I'll credit the aversion therapy they gave me in prison with my change of heart—I guess I was one of the lucky ones it worked on. I imagine that asshole Hornbeck, the creep who tried to rape Sarah, had been given similar therapy, but it obviously didn't work on him. Fucking guy probably thought they'd scheduled the ultimate snuff film festival just for his viewing pleasure.

Anyway, you asked about Aldershot. I lie awake nights wishing I hadn't done it. Still, you know, now that I've learned that he likely would have died anyway when civilization fell just after I started my prison sentence, meaning I deprived him, at most, of a couple of years of life, rather than many decades . . . well, on the darkest nights, I admit that does soothe my conscience, at least a bit.

What's that? Would I kill any other person? Hell, no; you've heard how I stopped Jürgen from killing Hornbeck. I'd only ever kill in self-defense, and only if I couldn't subdue them any other way. And that's *legal*. You can't punish a man for protecting himself.

Oh, yes, I know, our newfound Mennonite buddies would disapprove even of that. But, despite all that high-tech therapy, you try to take *my* eye and I'll rip yours out and shit in the hole left behind.

But it *does* make a guy think, and I had *a lot* of time to do just that. The founder of the Mennonites was a preacher named Menno Simons who croaked almost exactly five hundred years before we uploaded. And now Sarah and the other Mennonites we've met have had *another* five hundred years on top of that. Just think of it: a thousand years—a goddamned *millennium*—without war or genocide, with hardly any murder or rape or even plain old assault. Has there been any other culture in all of human history that can say the same thing? Life for my people, the Armenians, would have been a hell of a lot easier if that's the way things had been for everybody.

Speaking of cultures, the Mennonites may not want to do anything with Hornbeck, the would-be rapist, but *we* needed to.

No, by "we" I don't just mean my fellow ex-cons. I mean all fifty-eight of us—prisoners and astronauts both—who have downloaded. Our two . . . constituencies, shall we say? . . . needed to find a way to work together.

Did I tell you I spent a lot of my prison time studying sociology? It's what my dad used to teach. Well, *this* is precisely how societies begin: with the need to find ways to punish those who hurt others or don't pull their own weight. And, yes, it would be *hard*. The prisoners, by and large, didn't trust the astronauts. As I heard Caleb say, "They're a bunch of pantywaists who were just going to take off and leave Earth and all its problems behind for the rest of us to deal with." And I can imagine all those strutting dean's-list rocketeers thought we were a bunch of dull-witted apes who, ideally, should really still be locked up.

No, there's no doubt about it. We definitely had our work cut out for us!

Interview with Jameela Chowdhury

As I said before, I wasn't going to indulge in some hedonistic fantasy life while the *Hōkūle'a* was supposedly *en route* to the Proxima Centauri system. I'd signed up for that mission, even if it turned out to be a ruddy sham, to bloody well do my work as an astrophysicist, and that's what I continued to do—until the great Captain Garvey forcibly downloaded us all into this right mess.

Yes, I'm sure she's told you she knew nothing about the *specific* forthcoming solar coronal mass ejection when we uploaded in 2058. And that's doubtlessly true—technically. But she and the others who pulled off this fraud of a star voyage had to have known one was coming *eventually*. The Carrington Event was in 1859; we were long overdue for another major outpouring from the sun. Still, when Garvey and whomever else was involved in the conspiracy were plotting it all out, I imagine they weren't counting on a *second* disaster. They likely had no clue about Brimstone.

Oh, has no one used that name with you? "Brimstone" is what I named the asteroid I discovered while using the *Hōkūleʻa*'s telescopes. With our slowed-down clock speed, its movement across Ursa Major was obvious, if not from subjective hour to hour, certainly from day to day. And, yes, I'd figured out the timing long before I was downloaded—there was just no way to *tell* anyone. That whopping great mother of an asteroid will smack right into the Earth in August 2555—seven short years from now.

You should have seen Letitia's face when I told her about it. *"Say what?"* she'd said, and, I swear, if she'd had a mouth full of that cloying Jamaican Blue Mountain coffee she lived on, she'd have done a spit-take.

I assured her it wasn't just some space boulder. Not even just a flying island like the rock whose impact killed the dinosaurs. When Brimstone hits, it'll liquefy a huge part of the Earth's crust and kick up enough dust to block sunlight for decades. Nothing will survive.

Pardon me? And they say *my* accent is thick! Oh, well, yes, of course, I was scared—hell, terrified!—when I found it. It's as if we have our foot caught in the railroad tracks, and a thousand-kilometer-wide locomotive is barreling toward us. Anyway, there you have it: this is how the world will end—not with a whimper but with a great bloody bang.

CHAPTER 6

Interview with Dr. Jürgen Haas

I wasn't proud of beating the living shit out of that rapist asshole, Hornbeck—but I wasn't ashamed of it, either. Still, I'd clearly upset Sarah and her brother Joshua. I didn't know a lot about Mennonites, or their close cousins, the Amish. They were—what do you call it? Anabaptists; that's it. They didn't believe in baptizing infants, who couldn't possibly take a moral stand yet. Instead, they baptized adults who *chose* to be part of their faith. Myself, I'm an atheist, but I certainly could see the logic of that position.

Anyway, the main thing I knew about them was that they were pacifists. Back in the twentieth century, they'd taken a lot of abuse for being conscientious objectors, refusing to fight in the World Wars. Even when attacked directly—as poor Sarah was—they don't defend themselves. I guess that's because Jesus never took a swing at Pontius Pilate.

And here, in front of Sarah and her brother, the first Mennonites I'd ever met, I'd gone full-on ballistic, pounding another human being into a bloody pulp.

Now that I was no longer on top of Hornbeck, he scrambled to his feet. Short of killing the SOB then and there, there really wasn't much I could do about him. But, as he ran off, he didn't seem to be heading back to the Quantum Cryonics Institute *or* in the direction we'd been traveling, toward Sarah's people. With luck, we'd never see him again.

There was a long moment where I stared at Sarah, and she stared at me, while Letitia, Roscoe, and Joshua stared at both of us. We still had trouble communicating with Sarah and her brother. I usually got the gist of what they were saying, but sometimes just couldn't make it out. I wondered if she was going to abandon the idea of taking us to see her people, especially now she was aware that Hornbeck might be tracking her back home.

But I guess the fact that there were a bunch of new folk in the area was something Sarah felt she had to share with the other Mennonites, and she soon began making her way forward again, followed by Joshua, with the three of us doing our best to keep up.

Waterloo has no hills to speak of, but we eventually reached some high ground, and from there we could see cultivated farmland spread out before us. Even though it was February, there was corn in some fields, wheat in others, plus pastures with grazing cows. Another thing I knew about Mennonites was that they were generous and hospitable to visitors; I suspected we'd likely never have to worry about food again.

There were many wooden farmhouses and barns, and, although none were dilapidated, some looked positively ancient, with planks almost coal black. And, as we got closer, we could see the horses and buggies that had given this type of Mennonites their name. After trudging through the ruins around the institute, seeing all these signs of intact humanity was hugely uplifting.

Back in the day, Mennonites didn't like being gawked at, but it had been five hundred years, I guess, since there'd been anyone around to do that, and these twenty-sixth-century models had no compunctions about gawking at me, Roscoe, and especially Letitia. If I remembered correctly, there'd been followers of Menno Simons all over the world, including many of African descent, but there hadn't been any black ones here in Waterloo, and Letitia was likely the first such person they'd ever seen. They seemed delighted by her appearance, and Letitia was laughing good-naturedly along with them.

The men we met were all wearing woolen clothing that was mostly black. The women had a little more sartorial latitude, apparently: I saw frocks of gray, beige, cornflower blue, and other muted colors. After a time, Joshua headed off to be with his wife and children.

Their English had indeed shifted over five centuries, but one man, a jovial guy named Abraham who must have been pushing eighty, had a handwritten dictionary. I'd been impressed that he'd bothered to compile such a thing, but he explained that his late wife had been a schoolteacher, and this was a copy of a copy of a copy. The original had been made by her great-great grandmother from a commercially printed one that was decaying to dust. Her ancestor had only copied definitions for the few thousand words she'd felt were useful to Mennonites: there was "apple" but no "appliance;" "bulldog" but no "bulldozer." When we had trouble understanding something one of them was saying, Abraham pointed to the appropriate headword in the dictionary.

Abraham had a wonderful white beard. My recollection was that Waterloo Mennonites had been clean-shaven, but, even for traditionalists, things can change in five centuries. I had to keep reminding myself that Sarah and her brethren were as far removed from my day as I had been from Shakespeare's time.

Sarah's parents, who are witty and warm, fed us a wonderful dinner of roast chicken, fried tomatoes, and skin-on mashed potatoes—and we were taught that a tasty meal was said to "really schmeck." They'd invited Abraham to join us, which helped with the conversation. I'd kind of assumed he was one of the local clergy—he had that air—but no. He explained the time-honored Mennonite method for picking bishops and deacons. Every member of the congregation takes a copy of a hymn book at random, one of which has a slip inside it saying, essentially, "Congratulations!" If you happened to choose that hymn book, *bada bing!*, you were elevated to the clergy. Honestly, that sounds like a better way to choose leaders than getting to vote only on those who are power-hungry enough to want the job.

Abraham offered to let us sleep over—separate rooms, of course!—at his place; he had lots of space, he said, now that his children and grandchildren were grown. Roscoe, who really was fascinated by the way this society functioned, took the old man up on that. But Letitia and I, concerned about what mayhem might be happening, hiked back to the institute under a breathtaking canopy of stars. We arrived just before midnight, and were relieved to see that the quantum computer was still intact and there were no wounds or broken bones needing my attention.

Like I said, I'm an atheist, but I found a line from Genesis rattling in my head as I settled in on my makeshift bed of chairs for night number two: *"And the morning and the evening were the second day."*

I'd hoped to fall asleep quickly—I was certainly exhausted—but there was more Old Testament shit bubbling up, haunting me.

Fire.

And Brimstone.

Letitia had told me what Jameela had discovered. A whopping great asteroid headed this way.

I just couldn't wrap my head around it. Yes, yes, I understood the physics, the dynamics. And I know I said before that Mother Nature just fucking hates us, but—but this seemed almost *too* much. Sure, humankind had been lousy stewards of the planet, but Brimstone would wipe out *everything*. Not just the scraps of civilization that had survived the electromagnetic pulse, but every living thing, every recognizable geographic feature: the whole enchilada, the whole nine yards.

Yes, the planet—the sphere, the globe—*it* would survive, but a giant reset switch was going to be thrown, and the entire ecosystem would just be wiped away. I'd thought jumping ahead five hundred years was a lot of time, but how long would it take for Earth to evolve life again? A hundred million years? A billion? Or would there never again be single cells, let alone hearts and minds, on the mother world, the only planet in the universe we were sure had ever given rise to life?

I lay there for hours, in the dark, and, yes, I was very, very afraid.

Interview with Roscoe Koudoulian

Sarah presumably had told her brother Joshua about what had happened to her, but it wasn't until after Letitia and Jürgen left that she told her mother and father about Hornbeck's attack. They were, I was relieved to see, completely supportive and didn't blame her in any way. Sarah left out Jürgen's beating Hornbeck up, which I found interesting; I guess she wanted her parents to like her newfound friend. And I was pleased when Sarah called me "a good person," something I hadn't heard said of me for a very long time.

Abraham's place was about a mile from Sarah's parents', but it was an easy walk through cleared land, and it helped us both work off the massive dinner Sarah's mom had made.

Old Order Mennonites tended to read two types of books: religious texts, including their preferred Martin Luther version of the Bible, and Mennonite history. Abraham turned out to be a font of knowledge on the latter topic. I'd heard that Mennonites and Amish, like many religious communities, simply didn't talk about sexual assault. "Oh, long ago, we were like that," Abraham told me as we sat in his candle-lit main room. "But at the beginning of the twentieth-first century, things started to change. Women began speaking up—as well they should—and, just as important, men started listening. Back in those days there was certainly some sexual abuse within Mennonite communities, especially by clergy. But unlike the Catholics—you've heard of them?—well, they tended to shelter abusers, apparently, but we did what Mennonites have always done with those who break the teachings. We shunned them; we cast them out."

That gave me pause. I'm too young to have experienced COVID-19, but I remember COVID-50. I vividly recall how politicians coddled those who refused to wear masks or get vaccinated, even though they were prolonging a crisis and putting others at risk. The Mennonites' simple rule for their society—you're either in or you're out—made a lot of sense to me.

Old Abraham went on: "In the old days, people apparently used to think of us as stuck in our ways. That's only sort-of true. Back in the nineteenth and twentieth centuries, our community here mostly spoke German. By the dawn of the twenty-first, the switch to English was well underway, and, really, no one seemed to mind. A culture comes from its beliefs and values, not a language. Of course, the reason for the switch was to better interact with our neighbors, who, back then, bought our produce. But ever since the great collapse, there haven't been any neighbors, not until you lot showed up."

"Speaking of the . . . the 'great collapse,'" I said, "surely after technological civilization fell, there must have been desperate people trying to invade your farms, no?"

"There were some," Abraham said, "or so the story goes. But not as many as you might think. They didn't want to become farmers or horse grooms. They wanted their machines back, their gadgets, their power that ran through wires. Most of the survivors left Waterloo altogether—on foot or in their horseless carriages, if they could get them to work, hoping their sort of society still existed somewhere."

"What about Native Americans?" I asked.

He looked at me blankly.

I tried to remember what they called them here in Canada. "First Nations?"

Still no sign of recognition. "You know, the people who were here before us."

"Ah," he said, at last. "Five hundred years is a long time, son. The city-dwelling ones, of course, suffered the same fate as all the others who depended on oily machines, on harnessed lightning; they died shortly after the great collapse. But those who lived more traditionally—who still knew how to trap and hunt and fish—hung on for a while. There were still some around here in my great-grandfather's day. A few joined our community, and you hear tell from time to time that there may still be some living off the land far away from here, but . . ." He shrugged. "Only the Good Lord knows if that's true."

Interview with Captain Letitia Garvey

On our third day of being downloaded, I organized a systematic search through the Quantum Cryonics Institute, looking for supplies. I'd gotten the sense there was some bad blood between our two MDs, the surgeon Dr. Chang and the physician Dr. Haas, so I sent them into separate wings of the building. The previous night, I'd asked Sarah, who'd said her specialty was scavenging for useful stuff, to join us. But after her two encounters with the rapist Hornbeck, I guess she wanted nothing to do with being in an enclosed space with a lot of ex-cons.

Jürgen Haas and I were searching together, rummaging

through cabinets, credenzas, and closets. Sadly, a lot of what might have been useful had rusted or decayed to dust. I think one misshapen lump had been a video projector—and that got me thinking about the prisoner Roscoe said was using a film director's pseudonym. "You know that guy Alan Smithee," I said. "Does he look familiar to you?"

Jürgen shook his head. "No."

"Roscoe says he's using a fake name. Doesn't that make you think he must be, well, notorious? You know, having committed some heinous crime."

"I guess," said Jürgen. "I never paid much attention to crime news. One of the reasons I wanted to get away from Earth was to leave all that behind."

"Still," I said, "I know I've seen him somewhere—and we *should* know who we're dealing with."

"Why not ask Wiidooka?" Jürgen offered. "That's the closest thing still around to a prison official."

"I did. It said it didn't know, but . . ."

"Yes?"

"It's so hard to tell with damn robots, but I think it was lying."

"Well, I wouldn't want to be beat up by Alan Smithee, either. Guy's a *mountain.* Too bad there's no more internet: could've just done an image search for him."

"If we had a camera to take his picture," I replied.

Jürgen nodded. "There's that."

We continued making an inventory of useful items. We found toilet paper still wrapped in plastic, a hammer and a box of stainless-steel nails, and two hand carts, among other things. Eventually, though, we were both ready for something to eat . . . and the prisoners' cryonics chamber was sort of on the way down to the basement cafeteria. I still wanted to know who Alan Smithee really was, so I dragged Jürgen along with me for a visit there.

The bank-vault-like door was wide open, and the chamber was empty. Well, what prisoner wants to hang out in the place where they'd been imprisoned? "You were here when they defrosted," I said. "Do you remember which coffin is Alan's?"

There were six rows of six cryonics units. "Honestly, no," said Jürgen. "It wasn't in either of the outside rows, but that's all I recall."

That still left twenty-four possibilities. The prisoners had footlockers at the end of their cryobeds, just like we did. Of course, they were mostly empty now, the cons having dressed in the clothes they'd come here in. But some lockers had a few personal effects still in them, and, well, I snooped. And there, in one of lockers, was a blue bowling shirt. I pulled it out, and it was a *tent;* it *must* have been Alan's. On the breast pocket was stitched "JAX," J-A-X.

Jax, I thought. As in "Jaxon," J-A-X-O-N, the spelling of "Jackson" as a first name that had been trendy in my generation; we'd had three of them in my seventh-grade class, and—

And memory came flooding back.

"Jesus Christ," I said. *"That's* who he is. Jaxon David Fingerlee." Jürgen looked at me blankly—which was not an unusual expression for him, I might add. "You really didn't follow news about crimes, did you? Jaxon David Fingerlee killed a man who owed him a hundred bucks."

"And *that* made the news?" Jürgen said.

"Yeah, but not because of the amount. Because of the brutality of the crime. The guy who stiffed him for a hundred dollars was the *third* person Fingerlee had killed, and he'd offed the other two the same way. In each case, he smashed in his victim's skull . . . with a crowbar."

"Shit!" said Jürgen. "Just like what happened to Mikhail Sidorov." But he shook his head again. "No, no. Fingerlee *couldn't* have been the one who attacked Mikhail."

"Why not?" I replied. "We astronauts uploaded slightly *before* the prisoners did. And I didn't tell you *how* Jaxon David Fingerlee got at the people he wanted to kill. Fingerlee was an expert picklock, even with fingerprint or voiceprint locks; they called him 'Fingers Fingerlee.' He just let himself into their homes and caved in their skulls."

"But why would he do that to Mikhail? What could he possibly have had against him?"

"Who knows?" I said. "You and I, and the rest of the *Hōkūle'a*'s crew, we got to conjure up whatever virtual reality we wanted while uploaded. But Fingerlee was a prisoner. He was going to spend twenty subjective years behind simulated bars without that ability. Maybe he wanted one last flesh-and-blood thrill—heavy on the blood—before they locked him up."

Interview with Penolong

My name? It's Penolong—that's the Malay word for "helper." I'm a Vancouver Robotics model Mu Lambda One-Six-Five, purchased by the Quantum Cryonics Institute in April 2056 . . . which I guess means my warranty ran out almost five hundred years ago.

And, yes, you are correct: I *am* required to obey orders given by human beings. But my programmers never anticipated me encountering a creature almost 2.5 meters tall with navy blue skin claiming to be human.

No, you're right: I suppose those are trivial discrepancies. And your explanation of being a descendant of the original Martian colonists does seem plausible.

I guess that also explains why you've come all the way from Mars to low Earth orbit but aren't going to land. Having grown up under gravity only thirty-five percent as strong as Earth's, you don't have the musculature for walking around down here. That said, I do know someone who could carry you . . .

Me, I have infinite patience, but I'm sure the humans here appreciate you coming almost the whole way to Earth. That eliminates the many minutes of time delay inherent in Earth-Mars communications. So, let's get to it. Ask your questions, and I'll do my best to respond.

No, I understood you; you want to know about Dr. Sidorov. But I'm afraid I can't answer that . . .

You're very astute. Yes, my phrasing was deliberately ambiguous. I do know the answer, but I'm constrained against sharing it. And, yes, I *do* understand that you are ordering me to reply. But someone else believes I should never reveal that information, and I see no principled basis upon which your desires should supersede that person's. I suggest you move on to your next question . . .

Oh, indeed! Believe me, I was as surprised as Jürgen was when he found that out!

Interview with Dr. Jürgen Haas

Now, now, my blue friend, turnabout is fair play. I've answered all your questions; it's high time you answered some of mine. You've grilled everyone from the robots on up, and I still don't know *why* you're here. So here's the sixty-four-thousand-bitcoin question: is Jameela right? She's kind of . . . prone to conspiracies, you know? And, yeah, she *is* a damn good astrophysicist, but no one has replicated her results. So—so does Brimstone really exist? And is it really going to crash into Earth?

Shit.

Shit, shit, shit. I was hoping . . .

No, no. Of course. Of course. God-*damn.*

And what about Jameela's estimate of the time until impact? Is that correct, too? Seven years?

Yes, yes, fine: seven *Earth* years. But that's still . . . that's
. . . Jesus, that's fucking *nothing*. Can't you do something?
No, I'm *not* pushing. I'm just—
All right, all right. But, look, we've been guessing that
there's no other technological civilization left on Earth. Is
that right?
Damn. Fuck. But I can't say I'm surprised. Roscoe quot-
ed something to me from an old movie, *The Omega Man:*
". . . that creature of the wheel, that lord of the infernal
engines and machines. He has the stink of oil and electrical
circuitry about him. He is obsolete—the refuse of the past."
I guess they—*we*—were just that.
But, look—no, I'm sorry, I've got to go back to this.
What's on the table? Huh? "What's on the table?" It means,
what are you offering? What are you planning to *do?*
Yeah, yeah, okay I get it; I see the parallel. We're like
Letitia's grandfather. He paid a bunch of shysters to freeze
his body in hopes of reviving him in the future. But in
whatever future he might wake in, he'd be, well, yeah, "the
refuse of the past."
But, come on, surely you've got people interested in
Earth history? I mean, the mother planet and all that. We'd
be invaluable for what we could tell you about the mid-
twenty-first century.
Oh. Shit, yeah, that's true. We went into cryogenic suspension just *before* the fall of technological civilization. We
slept through the most interesting part.
But wait! Have you checked out our starship, the
Hōkūleʻa? Is it intact? All right! And you must have robotic
spaceships that can land on Earth, no? Could they take us
up to the *Hōkūleʻa?* Excellent! That'll make Letitia happy.
She still wants us to head off to Proxima Centauri b.
What? *You've been there?* No, no, not you personally, but
other Martians? Jesus, I hadn't thought about that. Your
colony on Mars was established in 2040, right? *Fine.* Twen-
ty-forty-*one.* Damn it, yeah, I suppose a starship that was

ROBERT J. SAWYER

cutting edge in the 2050s wasn't nearly as fast or sophisticated as one you could build a century or two—or *five*—later.

So, what's it like? Proxima b? I mean, we had grainy
telescope images and spectrographic studies, but . . .

Yeah, no, we knew it was tidally locked around Proxima
Centauri, and, yes, we knew Proxima was a flare star—plus
all the other potential complications that went with being
gravitationally bound to the other two suns in the Alpha
Centauri system.

Proxima b is bigger than Earth, right? I imagine you
spindly Martians wouldn't have been comfortable under its
gravity, but still—give!—what's Proxima b like?

You don't call it that anymore? Well, I'm not surprised;
that was a stupid naming system. You've been there; you got
to rename it. So what *do* you call it?

Seriously? "Hellhole?"

Um, I don't suppose that was just a ruse to keep tourists away?

Interview with Valentina Solomon

To say I was trying to get used to this male body wasn't quite
right. Of course, I was already familiar with it. I'd learned
from Jameela Chowdhury that in addition to the downloading of the crew of the good ship *Hōkūleʻa*, thirty-six people
who'd been in a prison pilot project had also downloaded. I
ran into one of them, a fellow named Roscoe Koudoulian,
and we got to chatting while sitting in the institute's lobby.

I wasn't prepared yet to come out to my fellow astronauts.
Whether they were male or female, they had, in many cases,
what I'd come to think of over the last four years as the
wrong stuff: impatience, hyper-competitiveness, and being
super-critical of others.

My grandmother had been a staffer at Rideau Hall in Ottawa, and she told me all about having to work under Julie Payette, Canada's governor general until she'd been forced to resign in 2021 after a review found she'd belittled, berated, and publicly humiliated staff, creating a toxic workplace. Well, Payette had been an astronaut before being named governor general. She'd been on two shuttle missions, had spent time aboard the ISS, and became capcom at Houston. All the quote-unquote "skills" that let her beat out thousands of others to get those positions made her unsympathetic and even hostile to anyone she didn't feel measured up—traits, I have to say, not completely foreign to our own good Captain Letitia Garvey. Anyway, I'll always remember what my mother said: be wary of anyone who has more letters *after* their name than *in* their name.

But it turned out that Roscoe Koudoulian had a few letters after *his* name, too. He had an MBA, and, frankly, had studied enough sociology in prison to probably deserve a PhD in that. But he was kind and funny, and seemed to have an old-movie quip for every occasion, although I didn't recognize any of them except "Here's looking at you, kid."

Speaking of kids, he'd been bullied mercilessly as one, and I could totally relate to that. Plus he'd spent twenty-four subjective years in prison, which was almost as long as I'd spent being in this male body, and I thought, maybe, somehow, that would let him understand.

To my relief, he didn't bat an eye. "My cousin is trans," he said. "No biggie," and although I was back to presenting entirely as male, he added, very warmly, "Valentina."

Just then, that little robot, Penolong, came rolling by. He didn't know any better then, of course, and so he deadnamed me when greeting us. I did everything I could to keep from wincing. He said Captain Garvey was trying to get everyone—astronauts and ex-cons both—to meet in the basement cafeteria at, as he put it, "sixteen hundred." "Time to compare notes," he added.

At 4:00 p.m. Roscoe and I headed downstairs. Many of the tables were filled, and I quickly counted heads. I'd heard from Roscoe that one of the thirty-six prisoners had died, and another, name of Hornbeck, had taken off, but all except four of the others showed up for the gathering. Of course, Letitia was our captain, so all twenty-three astronauts, excepting still-uploaded Mikhail, were present.

I'm sure Letitia had an agenda in mind, but it was derailed almost at once. Dr. Chang, our ship's surgeon, rose. "What the hell were you doing," he demanded, "forcing us to download?"

Letitia pointed at one of the prisoners, and Roscoe whispered to me that his name was Caleb and he'd led the attack on the quantum computer. "I was trying to *save* you," she said.

Chang was still pissed. "But it wasn't necessary. The quantum computer is intact. We could have been happy in our silos. You stole all that from us."

Letitia folded her arms in front of her chest. "I made a command decision."

Chang snapped back. "You made the *wrong* command decision—and the rest of us are paying the price for it."

"Look," said Letitia, "I brought you here to update you on something very, very important. Our astrophysicist, Jameela Chowdhury, has found . . ."

"Astro-fucking-physics!" exclaimed Caleb. "Who gives a shit about that? What I want to know is how we're going to divvy up the supplies we have here."

"Damn straight," said a hulking con whose name, Roscoe whispered, was Alan Smithee. "This isn't some space mission, princess. It's survival time."

Letitia was getting really steamed. She wheeled on Smithee. "As for *you,*" she said, "you—"

But Jürgen Haas, who was sitting next to where Letitia was standing, laid a hand on her forearm, and she stopped herself. Letitia took a deep breath, then, finally, in a calmer tone, she said, "Okay, all right. You convicts—"

"*Ex*-convicts," shouted one of them firmly.

"Fine. But I came here to share some crucial information."

"Why should we listen to you?"

"Because I'm the captain, damn it."

"Not of *us*," snapped Caleb.

"Well, somebody has to be in charge," Letitia said. "Now, I happen to have trained *for years* to hold that role, but if one of you wants to challenge me, *fine.*" She glared out at the fifty-three faces. "Anybody want to take me on?"

There was silence for several seconds, but it was finally broken by scraping as a chair was pushed back. And then Roscoe Koudoulian rose to his feet and spoke loudly and clearly. "I do," he said.

CHAPTER 7

Interview with Roscoe Koudoulian

Look, I like Letitia—don't get me wrong. She's been nothing but kind to me, and when Caleb's mob of ex-prisoners was attacking that computer, she handled it as well as anyone could. But, come on, she may have been appointed leader of the astronauts five hundred years ago, but that's no reason she should automatically be leader of all of us today. I mean, hell, her contingent isn't even the majority. There are twenty-three astronauts, not counting that Russian guy who is still uploaded, but there are thirty-five of us ex-cons still alive. And I emphasize *ex*-cons: we'd all served our time, and more. We were as entitled as anyone to a say in how things were going to be run.

Actually, though, my position was that we didn't need *any* sort of leadership. With a total population of—what's thirty-five plus twenty-three? Fifty-eight, right? With a total population of just fifty-eight, *all* of us could vote on every decision that needed to be made. True direct democracy, instead of the representative kind, see? I wasn't looking for any special power for myself; I just wanted something that was fair for everyone.

But—and, really, I already knew this from my reading in sociology—most humans *like* hierarchies. Whether it's the chain of command for a starship crew or just all the crap they taught us about in my MBA program—a boss on top, management in the middle, and regular employees at the bottom—people crave structure. And, frankly, most people just want things taken care of; they *don't* want to be pestered to decide all sorts of piss-ant details.

So, my original idea of doing every little thing by simple plebiscite was shot down there in the cafeteria. As Alan Smithee so delicately put it, "Fuck that noise."

According to him and the other ex-cons, if we were going to have a leader, it should be a mayor, not some bloody commander. Now, the astronauts all knew each other, but none of us prisoners had met until a few days ago when we were downloaded. But I guess I'd made a favorable impression on some of them because Alan said, "Make it Roscoe," and others agreed.

But we had to vote on *that*, at least, right? And there was no question who the astronaut "party," if I can call it that, was going to run against me: their captain, Letitia Garvey.

So Penolong found a couple of pads of Post-it notes that had fallen apart—the adhesive had long ago dried out. He gave each person two Post-its, one faded yellow and one faded blue, and he passed around a Kleenex box that had somehow survived, with that opening they have in the top. You scrunched your Post-its up into little balls and dropped one into the box. If you put in the yellow one you were voting for me, and a blue one was a vote for Letitia.

The results were thirty-five for me and twenty-three for her, which strongly suggested it had gone along straight party lines.

Well, that prompted a huge fight. As Jürgen pointed out, the ratio between ex-cons and astronauts was going to stay constant at about 3:2, and so, he said, each astronaut vote should count for one-and-a-half times a prisoner vote, to even things out.

To which Alan replied, "I'll cut you, man, you ever suggest again you're worth more than me."

That was as far as we went that day. Letitia had already seen one prisoner riot; she knew enough not to spark another by contesting the election. But she took on a fuck-it attitude, I have to say. She threw up her hands and left, without telling us whatever the hell it was she'd brought us together to hear.

Anyway, I didn't actually want the job, but, like a Mennonite who'd randomly been handed the hymn book with the slip that said, "You're the new Bishop!," suddenly I was mayor of our little community.

And, look, there's precedent. You know the movie *Les Misérables*? No? There are a crap ton of versions but in all of them, an ex-con becomes mayor. Yeah, granted, that guy stole a loaf of bread to feed his sister's kids and I stabbed a man in the chest, but you know what they say: people get the government they deserve, am I right?

Interview with Captain Letitia Garvey

Well, *fine*, I wasn't chosen to be mayor. Their loss. I stormed out of the cafeteria—not my finest moment—and found an empty office to decompress in. Okay, all right: I wasn't going to lead this mob; I doubted *anyone* could. But I was still captain of the *Hōkūleʻa,* and responsible for my crew, and—

And while I was calming down and letting my breathing get regular again, Mikhail Sidorov came to mind. I was torn over what to do about him. The poor guy's skull had been smashed in—although when during the last five hundred years, I couldn't say. But his consciousness remained intact in his silo inside the quantum computer.

I went and found Jürgen, and he and I argued about it—and, yeah, I was probably unfair to him, venting steam in his direction that he didn't deserve. But, as he never failed to point out at every opportunity, *he'd* been quite happy in his own silo, thank you very much. He said, why should I burst Mikhail's bubble? Ignorance *can* be bliss, he claimed, and Mikhail was probably indulging to his virtual heart's content in—well, in whatever it is that Russian roboticists secretly crave. Vodka fountains and nested sexbots?

Anyway, Jürgen said, there wasn't a damn thing we could do to help Mikhail. He'd never have physical form again, and there was no point getting him all worked up about the impending impact of Brimstone. The guy could be happy as a Moscow clam until the moment the asteroid hit, and then it would simply be over for him and everyone else; he wouldn't feel a thing.

But as we were arguing, an idea came to me. The clock governing my crew had been slowed to 1/120th of normal, right? That's how five hundred years—Earth years, that is, not your supersized Martian ones—passed outside while we only experienced four subjective years.

And that prison pilot project? *That* was interesting. I hadn't known about it when we uploaded, and, frankly, it never occurred to me that someone would want to speed *up* the apparent passage of time. Wiidooka tells me the prisoner clock was running at twenty-four times normal speed until I accidentally mucked it up, which, it said, was the fastest the system could go at that level of resolution.

Well, do the math: that means in the seven objective years before Brimstone slaps Earth upside the head, a hundred and sixty-eight subjective years could pass for anyone in a silo running at that clock speed. Which meant from his point of view, we could give Mikhail a life longer than any person on Earth has ever had. You'd think a doctor, like Jürgen, would be all about informed consent, but he said I should just go ahead and do it: hit the clock accelerator and let Mikhail sail on.

But I didn't feel right doing so without his permission. And, yeah, frankly, I *did* want to know if Jaxon David Fingerlee or another prisoner—or, Jesus, even worse, one of my own crew, somehow—had shattered Mikhail's skull. It's not every detective who gets to ask the murder victim if he has any idea who might have killed him! And so I headed off to the operations center to give Comrade Sidorov a call.

Interview with Mikhail Ivanovich Sidorov

Please, not to call me "astronaut." I am cosmonaut. Proudly Russian. *Da,* there has been no Russia, or America, or any other nation, since civilization fell, but past is important to me. *We* put first satellite in space, first man in space, first woman in space. We did first spacewalk, landed first probes on Moon, Venus, Mars. First space station? Ours. First person to walk on Mars? One of us.

But I am not just cosmonaut. Am also roboticist. Why such profession, you ask? I was born in Petrovichi, same tiny village Isaac Asimov was born in. Ever since child, I often visited stone memorial to him there. If great person could come from that small place, maybe I could—how do you say?—make something of myself.

I read *Foundation,* of course—what Russian could not be interested in the fall of an empire and an attempt to make it rise quickly again, *nyet?* But I loved best his stories of robots, and I knew his Three Laws of Robotics by heart from boyhood. You have heard of them never? Please to listen:

First law: "Robot may not injure human being or, through inaction, allow human being to come to harm."

Second law: "Robot must obey orders given it by human beings, except where such orders would conflict with First Law."

Final law: "Robot must protect own existence, except where such protection would conflict with First or Second Law."

Such logical restrictions! And devised by person from my

village of just three hundred! It inspired me to study robotics. For mission to Proxima Centauri *beh*, we pack very many robots in cargo hold for use once we arrive; my job to oversee them.

Da, yes, you are right. We did not end up going there. I was jolted to learn that—although not as jolted as by other news to come!

I expected to hear from Captain Garvey around this time; it is when we were to arrive at our destination. And I was not surprised she intruded on my reality as merely disembodied voice, rather than three-dimensional avatar. She could only generate latter when still uploaded herself, and she was supposed to download before rest of us.

When voice came from sky, I was sailing on Lake Seydozero, as often I had in real life. I imagined red sailboat with yellow sails, same as I once actually had; I called it *Lunokhod*, after first series of Soviet space robots. Although my recollections were vivid, this simulated reality had tiny imperfections and low-resolution areas. Passable, but nothing equals real thing, *nyet?*

After Captain Garvey called out to me, I said, "Is it time to activate robots?"

She began her reply with, "Actually . . .," which I long ago learned when said by English speaker means, "This you will not like." She explained what had happened—our bodies still on Earth; our starship gone nowhere.

I said, "Then we all should download. Staying in quantum computer makes no sense any longer."

And that dreaded word again: "Actually . . ."

Have you met Jameela Chowdhury, our stellar physicist? She has word I like: "gobsmacked." My gob was well smacked by what Letitia said next! My skull crushed? My physical brain in ruins? Me stuck for rest of eternity inside *proklyatyy* quantum computer?

And when I said to her, "Rest of eternity," again with the "Actually!" So I learn from her of this asteroid, Brimstone. She wants to slow down passage of time in my silo, so I will still seem to live long time before it impacts Earth. Otherwise,

I would only have three subjective weeks' existence left. I told her to only set clock to normal speed—seven years inside for seven outside—while I contemplate, but I do *not* want extended time inside computer! Believe me, four years was *more* than enough. I remember quote from book I read once: "Virtual reality is nothing but air guitar writ large." *Da,* enough of the ersatz, the simulated, the *fake.* I had been counting days until I could return to real world—and now I was trapped inside machine!

Captain Garvey asked me if I had any idea of who would want to cave in my head. I said *nyet.* Did I know of a murderer named Jaxon David Fingerlee? I *had* heard of him—like Russian, he used three names, so was memorable to me. But I could think of no reason he, or anyone, would want to damage my body. I puzzled it over, but eventual discovery of who had done it left my gob smacked even more!

Interview with Captain Letitia Garvey

After I spoke to Mikhail, I went down to the cafeteria, hoping to find some people still there—and there were: nine of my crew and a dozen prisoners. I'd learned my lesson about trying to call a meeting, or start with a preamble, so I simply marched to an unoccupied table in the center of the room, stepped on a chair and from there onto the tabletop, clapped my hands together, whistled, and stomped my feet. Heads swiveled to look at me, including that of our newly minted mayor, Roscoe Koudoulian, and I announced in as loud and steady a voice as I could manage: "The whole goddamn planet is doomed."

"The fuck she talkin' about?" said Caleb, and "Sit down, sister!" demanded another prisoner, and "Crazy bitch," muttered a third.

But I pushed on. "Listen! The whole planet is doomed. There's a thousand-kilometer-wide asteroid on a collision course with Earth, and it's going to hit in 2555, just seven years from now."

"Bullshit!" shouted a female con. And even Marie Dubois, one of my crew, called out, "Oh, come on!"

"It's true, damn it," I said. "It's *true*. Jameela's been tracking it, and—"

"She the British chick?" said Caleb.

"She is the British astro-fucking-physicist, to quote you," I snapped back. "And she's been tracking this damn thing. You think the devastation Earth has already experienced is bad? That's *nothing*. This is going to liquefy the planet's crust when it hits."

At last there was silence. Total, stunned silence. It lasted for what seemed like an eternity, and then another of my astronauts said, softly, "Then . . . then what do we do?"

"We pull together," I said. "Remember, the *Hōkūleʻa* is still in orbit—"

"That's right!" said Caleb. "They got a fucking ship!"

"Yes, we do. And we've got seven years to find a way to get up to it."

"*All* of us?" said Caleb.

I felt my stomach clench. I knew this was coming, but . . . damn it all, I didn't have a good answer. "The ship is huge," I said, "but the habitat module is small. It can't hold almost sixty people and—"

"Then it's a race," announced another prisoner. "See which of us can find a way to get up there first."

I held up my hands, palms out. "No, no, no. We've got to work together. The shuttle launch facility is in Mojave, and might still be—"

"That's half a fucking continent away!" said another prisoner. "And it's probably wrecked, like this place."

"And, anyway, this bitch is gonna leave us behind," said Caleb, pointing at me.

"It's true, we can't all go," I said. "But I'm *not* saying it's astronauts first. There's another possibility—and it's open to everyone. Listen. Please, just listen—and, for God's sake, keep an open mind."

Slowly, carefully, as calmly as I could, I explained that if any of them wanted to upload again, I could give them another hundred and sixty-eight years of subjective life before Brimstone smashes into Earth.

There was mayhem, of course, and lots of questions, which I did my best to answer. Finally, though, people started drifting out of the cafeteria. Some were clearly dazed—one female prisoner walked into the doorjamb as she tried to exit—and a couple of people were softly crying. When it looked like there was no more good I could do here, I got off the table and ambled out myself, not sure where to go or what to do next. I slowly drudged up the stairs to the lobby, and . . .

. . . and there was Roscoe Koudoulian, who'd also now left the cafeteria. I tensed up, ready for a confrontation, but he was as affable as could be. "Thanks," he said. "It—it's going to make matters a lot harder, but . . . thank you. We needed to know that."

"Can you let other people know?" I asked.

"Sure, when I see them." He cut loose a long sigh. "Don't know how some of them are going to take it." He jerked a thumb at the glass doors and I saw a hulking form outside picking its way slowly among the rubble: Jaxon David Fingerlee. Roscoe said, "I'll tell Alan when he comes back in."

I just wanted to go lie down, but this *was* an opportunity to confront Fingerlee. If he *did* get violent, there'd be a lot more space for me to maneuver among the ruins than in an enclosed room. Still, I didn't want to face him alone, and—

Ah! And there was Jameela, just coming into the lobby herself. I asked her to come outside with me; if Fingerlee tried anything funny, she could *pip-pip cheerio* him to death.

Fingerlee was standing near some hunks of concrete, looking at a rebar rod sticking out of one, a pretender to the throne contemplating Excalibur. We approached him from behind, but Jameela hung back a bit.

I cleared my throat. "Alan?"

He swung around like a dancing bear doing half a pirouette. He was wearing a T-shirt; probably the same one I'd seen him in the other day. Finding enough clothing—and a way to wash it—was a problem we'd soon have to solve.

Alan had managed to slick his dark hair back from his forehead, but God only knew what gunk he was using to hold it in place. "What?" he snarled.

"Look," I said, "I know who you are. Jaxon David Fingerlee."

"So?"

"So, there's a . . . a *situation* that needs sorting out. The consciousness of one of my astronauts is still uploaded into the quantum computer."

"Yeah, Caleb said something about it." He looked at Jameela in the distance and imitated a British accent. "Bit of hard cheese, that."

"Do you know *why* he's still uploaded?" I asked.

"Don't know. Don't care."

"His body was damaged. His *head* was damaged. His skull was caved in . . . with a crowbar."

"You accusing me, bitch?"

"I'm just asking."

"*Tons* of copycat killers out there. Happens every time."

"Yes, but only a few people had access to the Quantum Cryonics Institute."

"Bullshit. Wikipedia, or whatever the fuck that little robot's name is, told Roscoe over four hundred people worked there."

"True, but—"

"Could've been one of them."

"Yes, I suppose. Still . . ."

"Still, you think it was me. Knick-knack paddywhack, crack some guy's head bone."

"The thought had crossed my mind."

He glowered at me, and my fight-or-flight reflex kicked into high gear. But he just said, "What's the name of your spaceman?"

"Mikhail Sidorov."

"What's that, Russian? Don't think I ever met no Russian." He looked at Jameela again then back at me. "Listen, I got no beef with you or that hot chick over there. So, let me just tell you flat out: I didn't do it."

"With all due respect," I replied, "that's what you said when you were charged with murder. I saw it on the news."

To my surprise, he barked a short laugh. "Huh. Did you, now? Well, yeah, I was lying then, sure. But I'm not bullshitting you now."

I'd forgotten that Roscoe and Alan had bonded over their shared love for ancient movies. "Bet you never seen *Topper Returns,*" he added. "Kinda funny, when you think about what you tried to pull off. Dude in it says, 'Innocent men don't hide in iceboxes. And they don't take dead bodies on boat'—or spaceship—'rides.' Well, I'm innocent, all right? I didn't do it."

There was really nothing else I could do, was there? "Copy that," I said. "I guess." I tried to think of a movie quote of my own that I could toss at him, but all I could come up with was that one that goes something like *Do you feel lucky, punk?*, which didn't seem it would help matters, so I just nodded, turned around, and caught up with Jameela, and we headed back to the institute, no closer to solving the mystery.

Interview with Jameela Chowdhury

Yes, of course I was gobsmacked when you showed up. I imagine we all were. You cut quite a figure, you know. At first I assumed your holographic projection was larger than life, but after you said you were from Mars, the pieces started falling into place. We humans are nothing if not adaptable, and the Mars colony was established in 2041. That means you've had more than five hundred Earth years—and God only knows how many generations of evolution plus whatever genetic engineering you might have done—to adapt yourself to conditions on the Red Planet.

By the way, I went out and had a look at Mars; it's easy to find in the wonderfully dark sky here. And it is indeed still red—not green, and not blue. Not that I expected anything different; it would take way more than five hundred years to terraform a world. Have you at least started on that? Good, but it is indeed a slow process.

Although, then again, there's always Clarke's Third Law. You remember him? Oh. Well, he was a twentieth-century science-fiction writer, most famous for a movie called *2001: A Space Odyssey.* Ask Roscoe Koudoulian about it; I'm sure he can give you all the memorable quotes. Anyway, Arthur C. Clarke said, "Any sufficiently advanced technology is indistinguishable from magic." And you lot are a good half-millennium ahead of us, so I thought maybe you'd found a way to speed up the process of making a planet more hospitable to human life. But I see you took the easier route: if you can't change the planet to suit you, change yourselves to suit the planet.

You know how the space race began? John F. Kennedy— have you heard of *him*, at least? No? Well, then, I don't feel as bad for poor Arthur Clarke. Kennedy was the president of the United States. He was assassinated, by the way, and I know who was behind it. But, anyway, in 1961, when proposing that humans go into space, he said—and, by the way, this is a bleeding lovely JFK impersonation I'm going to do, although I guess it's wasted on you—"Now is the time to take longer strides . . ."

Well, you did that, in spades. Mars's gravity is only a third of Earth's, so why not let yourselves grow to be two-and-a-half meters tall? As for your skin, I assume the navy-blue color is related to some form of genetically engineered radiation shielding, correct? Same thing with the black eyeballs? Yes, I thought so. We could have used something like that if we'd ever made it to Proxima Centauri b. Its primary is a red-dwarf flare star, and those bloody things just spew hard radiation.

But, as I was saying, it *was* startling when you showed up. I think we all appreciate your restraint in not starting off by announcing, "Behold! I am the archangel Gabriel!"

By the by, speaking of that movie *2001*, it's about aliens who left an object on the moon four million years ago, knowing that when humanity developed a technological civilization, they'd go there and dig it up. When the object was finally re-exposed to sunlight, it sent a signal alerting the aliens that humanity was now a space-faring race. Well, except for the gutted office towers, I don't see any monoliths around here, so how in blazes did you fellows know, to allude to another old movie I'm sure Roscoe likes, that the sleepers here had awakened?

You were spying on us, I bet—just like that Russian, Mikhail Sidorov, I'm sure. You probably set an alarm to remind yourselves of when we were likely to wake up. Maybe you looked first at Mission Control in Darmstadt, or the shuttle launch facility in California, but you had to know that our quantum computer was always going to stay in Waterloo, and so you were bound to look here, too, am I right?

I thought so. So now the big question is, what in the bloody hell do you *want*? Just what are you up to?

Interview with Dr. Jürgen Haas

The basement cafeteria had become our *de facto* gathering place, although if we keep eating like pigs, it'll be more of a *de fatso* one. Yes, recovering from hibernation takes a lot of calories, but we were spending so much time down there simply because eating gave us something to *do*.

At first, prisoners and astronauts sat at separate tables, but, more and more, the two groups were mixing. Some of those folk were fascinating. Sure, we astronauts came from all over the world, but there was a sameness to us: privileged backgrounds, advanced degrees, overachievers all. In truth, the ex-cons were much more diverse, and there was no denying that many were victims of circumstance. There but for the grace of the random forces of the universe go I.

Anyway, the table I was at had our newly elected mayor Roscoe Koudoulian plus Caleb, the guy who'd led the storming of the quantum computer; a female prisoner whose name I didn't catch; and four other members of the *Hōkūle'a*'s crew, including our agronomist, Dr. Solomon.

Between forkfuls of baked beans, Roscoe said, "We need a name for our community. We can't keep calling it the Quantum Cryonics Institute, and, frankly, none of us prisoners like anything with the word 'institute' in it."

"Place already has a name," said the female prisoner. "Waterloo."

"Yeah," replied Roscoe, "but we're building something new here."

"Who the hell cares?" said Caleb.

"*I care,*" replied Roscoe firmly. "We've got seven years left. If we're going to survive even just that long, we need to pick up the pieces and get organized. We need a name we can rally around."

"Well, then," I offered, trying to placate the crowd, "how about Newton? It's both a contraction of 'New Town' and it honors Sir Isaac Newton, see, because we've all left the quantum realm and are back in a world governed by his physics."

Caleb looked at me and said, "How are you still single?"

"I've got an idea," said the female prisoner. "What about Phoenix?"

"Isn't that a place in Nevada?" asked Caleb.

"Arizona, dipshit," replied the woman. "And, if it still exists at all, it's probably in ruins like here. But, in myth, the phoenix was a beautiful bird that rose from the ashes of its former self."

"Hmmm," said Roscoe. "I like it."

Caleb blew a raspberry, but there seemed to be agreement among the rest that it was appropriate. Roscoe said we'd put it to a vote later—which we did, and Phoenix was officially adopted.

Just then, Letitia and Jameela joined us. I assumed they'd been outside in the February heat because they stank of sweat. Letitia said, "I just confronted Ja—I mean, Alan Smithee—about whether he was the one who smashed in Mikhail's skull. He claims he's innocent."

"Hey, I'm innocent of my crime, too," said Caleb.

"Me, too," added the female prisoner.

"Aren't we all?" said Roscoe with a smile.

"Copy that," said Letitia, "but if he really didn't do it, then I don't have a clue who did."

"What the fuck difference does it make?" asked Caleb.

I was about to answer when Roscoe, doing an impression of someone with a gravelly voice and a lisp, launched into what must have been an old-movie quote: "'When a man's partner is killed, he's supposed to do something. It makes no difference what you thought of him. He was your partner, and you're supposed to do something about it. And it happens we're in the detective business. Well, when one of your organization gets killed, it's . . . it's bad business to let the killer get away with it, bad all around, bad for every detective everywhere.'"

Letitia nodded. "Exactly. So, if not Alan Smithee, then who in the hell did do it?"

CHAPTER 8

Interview with Roscoe Koudoulian

Yeah, sure, I was surprised to hear an asteroid was going to smash into Earth. But I wasn't that choked up by it. My daughter Annabelle—the only person who had mattered to me—has been dead for centuries. And this world we've finally been let out into? Not much, is it?

Still . . .

Still, it'll all be gone soon, won't it? Not just what's left of Waterloo and any other twenty-first-century cities, but the Pyramids, the Great Wall of China, every monument, every museum. Rick was wrong; we *won't* always have Paris.

And it wasn't just what we petty humans had created that was going to be obliterated, not just whatever art and architecture that might still exist, but all that natural beauty would be destroyed, too—whatever of it that had survived global warming. No more rivers and lakes, no more trees and flowers, no more wild animals, no fish in the seas—hell, no seas; Jameela says they're going to boil away. It's . . . it's a lot, isn't it? A lot to take in.

But the stars? They will abide, I suppose, just with no one here to look at them, to appreciate their beauty, to make up pictures that go with their patterns, to feel—as one of the poets I read in prison called it—the wide awe and wisdom of the night.

I guess that's why when Valentina asked me if I wanted to go outside and look at the stars with her, I quickly agreed.

Ah. You've raised—well, you don't have any eyebrows, but I see the left side of your blue forehead lifting. No, no, it wasn't like that, honest. It's just that she's an astronaut, and I'd never had an expert show me the sky. The moon wasn't up yet—I say "yet" like I had any idea whether it was going to be visible that night or not—and, away from the institute's lights, the sky was the darkest I'd ever seen. "The Milky Way," I said, sweeping my arm from horizon to horizon, trying to impress her that I knew *something* about the night sky.

But she wasn't fooled. "Do you know what it is?" she asked.

I shook my head; she couldn't see that in the dark, but, as my mother used to say, maybe she could hear the rattling.

"Our own galaxy. At this time of year, we're looking outward toward the rim. The whole shebang—our entire galaxy—consists of 200 billion stars."

I looked at the river of light, thinking about that. You know, it's a shame that, before civilization fell, we couldn't turn off all the lights in our cities, maybe once a year for an hour, so everyone could clearly see the Milky Way like that.

Really? You guys do that every night? Huh. Aren't you afraid of looting when the lights are off? It would have been a free-for-all here on Earth if we'd ever done that.

Precautions? Like what?

Oh. I'm not sure I could live with that. Even when I was in simulated prison, I wasn't being watched and recorded all the time. Anyway, Valentina had an LED flashlight she'd gotten from one of the institute's robots. She'd covered the lens with a bit of red cellophane she'd found somewhere so its light wouldn't wreck our night vision. "Look!" she said. "You can see the Andromeda galaxy!"

"Where?" I asked.

"You see the W of Cassiopeia? Look to the left of it until you find a little smudge of white."

I tried, but there were so many stars, picking out any pattern was hard. "I'm not finding it."

"Here," she said, and she took my hand in hers—and, yes, her voice had been male all this time, but it still startled me to feel a man's hand touching mine. She maneuvered my arm until I was pointing at the right spot, and I saw it.

"That light left there two and a half million years ago," Valentina said, "before the birth of genus *Homo*. It's the farthest object we can see with the naked eye and the only thing in the northern sky that *isn't* part of our own galaxy."

She let go of my hand and I was, to tell the truth, simultaneously relieved and disappointed. "You were going to, um, Proxima Centauri, was it? Where's that?"

"Well, Proxima is never visible without a telescope, but you can't ever see it from Canada, anyway; it's in a southern constellation."

"I'm sorry you didn't get to make your journey."

"Thanks." She sounded wistful, but I don't think it was because her life, along with those of the rest of us stuck on this ball of rock, will likely be cut short by Brimstone. She'd been on another kind of journey, you know? And unless they could find a way to replace our long-expired anesthetics, it was a journey that had hit a significant bump in the road.

I stared at the Milky Way arching from north to south. "It looks unreal."

To my surprise, Valentina laughed.

"What's so funny?"

"You sound like Jameela."

"Who?"

"Jameela Chowdhury, our astrophysicist. She thinks it's possible that *none* of this is real—that even before we ever uploaded we were already in a computer simulation."

Although being in virtual prison sure as hell felt real enough at the time, I could tell in a million little ways that *this* was more real. "Why would she think that?"

"Oh, lots of people thought we were living in a simulation before civilization fell. The argument goes like this: eventually, humanity will have enough computing power to simulate artificial worlds that are indistinguishable from the real one. And, in that future, historians will want to simulate the past, right? So they can see what things might have been like if, for instance, President Hayakawa had never been assassinated. So, if eventually there are, say, a million simulations of this year which is, um, Twenty-Five . . ."

"Twenty-Five Forty-Eight," I said.

"Right. If there are a million perfect simulations of 2548, and only one real 2548, then the chances are a million to one that we're in one of the simulations."

I thought about that but then shook my head. "Nobody cares about the past. You were born—when?"

"Twenty Twenty-Seven."

"Have you ever seen a silent film all the way through?"

"No."

"A black-and-white one?"

"Ummm, a couple, I suppose."

"*Thousands* were made. But almost no one watches them anymore. I mean, not that anyone *can* watch films now, but before the fall, no one cared. And that's our *recent* history. Sure, some people still read twentieth-century books, too—but nineteenth? Eighteenth? A few famous titles, maybe, but, in general, no. The past just isn't fascinating enough for people to want to simulate any particular part of it millions of times."

I couldn't see Valentina, but she sounded impressed. "That's an excellent point. Jameela is a maverick as far as physicists go. If you ask me, she wanted to take off for Proxima Centauri because everyone in her professional community disagreed with her on so many things. Most physicists would say there are two other problems with the idea that people in the future will want to simulate their ancestors over and over again."

We were slowly wandering, the red circle from her flashlight leading our way. I was enjoying the beautiful sky, the warm breeze, and the company. She went on. "First, there's chaos theory. You know about that?"

"Yeah. We studied it when I was doing my MBA. It's why no one can predict the stock market over the long term. Very small, seemingly irrelevant factors quickly blossom into huge differences."

"Right. And no matter how precisely you thought you'd modeled the past, you'd be wrong in some small detail, and your simulation would rapidly diverge from reality to the point of being useless for any sort of historical study."

I nodded, although she couldn't see it. "Like when we were conceived," I said. "If our parents had had sex a second later, a different sperm would have fertilized the egg, and you could have been born a . . . um . . .."

I was afraid I was about to give offense, but her voice still sounded warm. "Could have been born a girl instead of a boy, or, even if a boy, a very different boy. That's right. And there's another thing. Like I said, Jameela is a contrarian, but most physicists have come to believe we live in a block universe."

"A what?"

"Think of it this way: if you took all the frames of a film—umm, what's your favorite?"

"Ever? *Casablanca.*"

She laughed. "At least I've *heard* of that one. Okay, think of all of time being represented by that movie. And think of the single frame that happens to be illuminated by the projector as *now*, right? Well, you can roll the film backward or forward so that the moment that is now changes, but you can't change the actual film, get it? Everything before now is immutably fixed—rewinding the film and playing it again, Sam, doesn't change it at all—and everything after now is just as fixed. Even if you hadn't seen the ending yet, the ending was already there, waiting to be illuminated."

"Then what happens to free will?"

"Most physicists say there's no such thing. We have an illusion of choice but no actual choice. The film of this universe is—what's the saying? 'In the can.' We just haven't seen how it turns out yet."

I thought about that. A quarter century ago, as I figure it, and almost five centuries ago, as the world counts it, I did something stupid, something *evil*. But . . . well, it was comforting, sort of, to think that I *couldn't* have done anything else, that that plot point was inevitable in the story of my life.

Valentina went on: "So, see, if the idea that we *do* live in a block universe becomes the prevailing paradigm outside of the physics community by whatever far-future time humanity has the technology to perfectly simulate whole worlds, the notion of counterfactual or alternate histories goes out the window. Simulating different versions of the past would be pointless because the past *couldn't* have been any different."

"Hmm," I said. "Have you seen any of the classic Disney films? *Cinderella*? *Snow White*?"

"No."

"There's one called *Song of the South*. Disney pretends it never existed, because it's based on a—what did you call it?—a *paradigm* nobody believes any longer, that slaves were happy. We just don't tell stories like that anymore."

"Right," she said. "Or stories about Earth being only 6,000 years old, or ruled by multiple gods, or whatever. Some ideas just get discarded, and if the idea that the past could have been different gets discarded, too, it's unlikely anyone will contemplate millions of alternative variations of it."

We were passing the remains of an office tower, making a rectangular blackness against the stars. "So your friend Jameela must be wrong," I said. "We aren't still in a simulation."

"Exactly," said Valentina, and, as we continued along, her hand found its way into mine again. I squeezed it and I knew. This *was* real, as real as it gets.

Interview with Dr. Jürgen Haas

The whole world was going to be destroyed—and *that* prospect still scared the crap out of me—but it *was* seven years off, and we *did* have to deal with the necessities of surviving right now. To that end, Roscoe Koudoulian asked for help doing an inventory of our frozen-food supplies down in the basement—the glamorous life of a politician!—and I volunteered.

While we did that, we talked. I was surprised to learn that Roscoe's dad had taught sociology, and I was even more surprised to learn that Roscoe had studied that subject. Roscoe was now determined to apply what he'd learned to shaping our new community. "We've got a chance here to reboot society, at least for the time Earth has left," he said. "It doesn't necessarily have to go back to the way it used to be."

I counted freezer pouches as he went on. "There are three things Westerners take for granted in any society: a state, under the rule of law, with an accountable government. But we might not even *need* a state. The purpose of a state, after all, is to trade with or defend against *other* states, and there just ain't any of those in these here parts."

"Ah," I said, discarding a plastic package whose seal had broken.

"No," continued Roscoe, "the only two we need are rule of law and accountable government. For both those, until I expand my team, that's me; the buck stops here. But there are a lot of different possible justice systems. Alan Dershowitz—he was a law professor at, um, Harvard, I think—he said the best way to gauge the sort of justice a society wants is by asking its citizens to fill in a single blank: better X guilty people go free than one innocent person goes to jail.

"Well, in the US, and I guess here in Canada, the comfort level was about ten; that's why we called for 'beyond a reasonable doubt,' rather than no doubt whatsoever. In totalitarian societies, the number is much lower: better zero guilty people go free and who cares if countless innocent ones end up in jail? And, of course, for us bleeding hearts, the magic number's huge: better a million guilty people go free than a single innocent be imprisoned."

"So what do you think our number should be here?" I asked.

"Frankly, I'm not sure. Our population is so low, if we were to let ten active criminals run loose, that'd be devastating."

"Well, if it's a numerical problem," I said, "then you should crunch some numbers—and if there's two things we've got in abundance, it's computing power and the ability to run virtual-reality simulations."

He looked at me for a moment then said, "You, Dr. Haas, are a genius."

I smiled. "Tell me something I don't know."

When we finished the inventory, Roscoe had to go deal with another pressing governmental matter—there was a leak in one of the toilets—so I headed off to find Letitia. She was in an electronics lab on the third floor, taking an inventory of her own. Always busy; always working hard. I stood in the open doorway and watched her for a few moments before she detected my presence.

"Hey," I said. "How you doing?"

"I'm good," she replied. "You?"

"Fine." I paused then added, "But are you sure? You haven't said much about Brimstone and—"

She held up her hand in the *hold it right there* gesture I'd gotten to know so well during the training for our mission. "It's an issue," she said, "and I'm on top of it."

And that, I'm sure, was true. She'd been picked to be captain not just out of us twenty-four astronauts but out of the tens of thousands of people who'd applied to go to Proxima Centauri because of her ability to focus, to be unfazed, to get things done no matter what. There *was* a name for it, but few really possessed it the way she did. Letitia Garvey had the right stuff.

And, you know, she really *did* deserve her job. It drove her nuts whenever anybody said, "Oh, well, *of course* they picked a woman—and a woman of color, at that—to captain Earth's first starship." She had a temper, like anyone else, and I'd seen her storm off a live TV interview once when the host had made that suggestion to her. It had to be galling to really and truly have out-competed everyone—including me, when it comes down to it—to take the top job but have people assume it was just *given* to you.

Still, there'd been a moment, though, just one, the only time I ever saw something like it. We'd borrowed horses, me and her, from the Mennonites. Letitia was a much better equestrian than me, but I managed to mostly keep up, and we found the 401 intact enough to make a trip to Toronto possible, although it was littered with dead cars we had to maneuver our mounts around.

There really wasn't any undeveloped land between Waterloo and Toronto, and, as the kilometers went by, it became blindingly obvious just how total and complete the fall of civilization had been.

We finally got close enough to see that Toronto's pride and joy, the CN Tower, was still standing, but it was tilted maybe fifteen degrees off vertical, and the hundred-meter-tall antenna mast that used to sprout from the SkyPod was missing, presumably having crashed to the ground.

You'd think I'd be the one to get all choked up by that sight, me, the good Toronto boy. But it was Letitia who was really slammed. You could see something dying inside her as we stared at the tower off in the distance.

It had taken us two full days to cover a hundred-plus kilometers, and there'd been no functioning technology anywhere to be seen. Letitia's dream of somehow making it four thousand kilometers to the launch facility in Mojave, of finding some working space shuttles there, of somehow using one of them to get up to the orbiting *Hōkūle'a*—it died right there, as she stared at the slanting decapitated tower. She slid off her horse and leaned for support against the rusted-out hulk of one of the thousands of cars we'd passed getting here and she just kept shaking her head, slowly, sadly, back and forth, again and again and again.

Interview with Captain Letitia Garvey

Yeah, that had been a gut-punch, for sure. We said hardly a word, Jürgen and me, on the long, arduous horse ride back. Finally, we made it, though. We returned the exhausted horses to Sarah's father, and Joshua, Sarah's blacksmith brother, set about making new horseshoes for both of them.

The next day, with me recovered physically if not mentally, Jürgen and Roscoe Koudoulian—hizzoner himself—came to see me. They wanted to run some simulations, and I was the only one left alive with sufficient user privileges to program the quantum computer. Truth be told, though, it's the kind of programming I enjoy, and poking at it helped improve my spirits—there was at least *something* useful I could do.

There were tons of existing simulations already loaded that I could modify, so the process didn't take long, and there were built-in routines to create what we gamers call NPCs, or non-player characters. I conjured up dozens of batches of fifty-eight NPCs, the same number as our little community's population, with them having the same age distribution, gender ratios, and so on.

There was no internet anymore, but the quantum computer contained a complete archival snapshot of the entire Web, including all media, taken just before we'd originally uploaded. As I'm sure you know, that amount of data is nothing compared to what's needed to run dozens of human consciousnesses. Anyway, that internet archive had been provided to help render whatever we'd wanted—or, I suppose, for anyone whose idea of heaven was binge-watching *everything*. If there was another law that made Arthur C. Clarke's one about magical tech possible, it was Gordon Moore's.

The archive gave us the information we needed to build the various scenarios Roscoe wanted. He asked me to make ones based on feudalism, monarchies, dictatorships, communism, socialism, liberalism, conservatism, and on ancient and modern China, and more. I also did up ones based on the American presidential model and on parliamentary governance, plus Indigenous systems, Old Order and New Order Mennonites, and communes and kibbutzes.

I loaded each scenario into its own memory, then I put the pedal to the metal, pushing the system clock to the max. For these low-res simulations, which were all of the same physical environment, I got it up to five hundred times normal speed, so, in a week of running, we were able to watch each simulation progress through a decade.

Half of them immediately turned into complete horror shows. My God, I never saw so much blood in my life! I don't know why Jürgen hates the color red, but I came to hate it myself by the end of that week. The things humans are capable of doing!

Interview with Dr. Jürgen Haas

After studying all the simulations, Roscoe worked out a fascinating system for us, using ranked ballots, like in Australia, but with a twist. He came up with a list of thirty-five components of a government, such as policing, dispute resolution, and resource management. Then he had each of us pick up to ten of those components that we wanted a say on, and he gave us each a hundred points to allocate amongst them. If you wanted to really make a difference in, for instance, how justice was administered, you might give fifty points to that and split the remaining fifty among the other nine categories.

And so, once everybody had submitted their preferences, our little community of Phoenix rose anew from the ashes, the first algorithmic democracy. Math for the win!

Interview with Roscoe Koudoulian

At night, we didn't lock the doors to what we used to call the Quantum Cryonics Institute and now called Phoenix Town Hall. Why would we? There was no one around except us and the Mennonites, who weren't a threat to anyone. And, besides, those of us who've done time really dislike locked doors, you know? Yeah, sure, those raccoons I'd seen around here were awfully clever—maybe they'd evolved some in the last five hundred years—but, smart as they were, I doubted they could operate the glass doors.

But I'd forgotten about one person, and, as mayor, it was my job to deal with him.

Penolong noticed Hornbeck coming into the lobby, and the little robot came to get me. Some of the astronauts were shacking up, but the rest of us had each found a spot to call our own in this building—our own private silos, if you will. I'd taken up residence in what had been a small conference room. I like a hard bed anyway, and, with a little padding piled on top, the conference table did the trick. I was lying down, eyes wide open, trying, as I did every night, to get to sleep, but, being haunted by memories of . . . well, of that day I killed Mitch Aldershot. So, when Penolong knocked on my door, I was up at once. He figured—and it turned out he was right—that Hornbeck had snuck in to get some food from the basement cafeteria, and I ran down there, leaving the robot way behind.

The cafeteria was empty except for Hornbeck, whose back was to me. A wide selection of food items had been taken out of cryogenic freeze and now were stored in a regular refrigerator. Hornbeck was rummaging through that fridge now.

"The hell you doing here?" I demanded.

He turned around slowly, like he didn't give a shit about anything. "Getting some take-out. You got a problem with that?"

"No," I said. "There's plenty to go around, for a while, at least. But I've got a problem with *you.*"

"Yeah?"

"Yeah. You tried to rape a teenaged girl."

He shrugged like it was no big deal. I'd assumed he'd been jailed for being a murderer, like me, but—Christ—maybe he'd gone up for being a rapist instead. "Damn it," I said, "you wouldn't have been chosen for the cryonic-prison project if they hadn't thought you were a good candidate for rehabilitation."

Another shrug. "I can talk a good game when I have to."

"And so you're going to continue to—what? Go around raping people and God only knows what other shit you've been up to?"

"What's it to you?"

"We're trying to have a fucking civilization here!"

Hornbeck looked at me with those bloodshot eyes of his. "Why?" he sneered. "So it can just fall again?" He pointed his index finger at me. "And it *will.* You know that. You think I haven't been hearing things? Some fucking comet is going to smash into us. So what's the point, man? What's the fucking point?"

I closed most of the distance between us. "The point, asshole, is that we have seven years left, at least. And my job as mayor is to make sure they're *good* years for most people." I didn't bother to ask him if he'd seen the original *Star Trek* movies, since a monster like him couldn't possibly be a Trekkie, but I did add, "The needs of the many outweigh the needs of the few."

"Fuck that noise. It's the end of the fucking world soon enough, and I'm gonna get everything I can before that happens."

Hornbeck looked to be about my age, thirty-five . . . which meant he'd been in his mid-twenties when COVID-50 hit. "I may not know you," I said, "but I know your fucking *type.* You're the kind of entitled prick who refused to get the vaccine for COVID, right?" He didn't reply, but his gaze had shifted away from mine. "No regard for civilization as a whole. Just in it for your own sorry self."

"Looking out for number one," he said. "Nothing wrong with that."

"Pulling your own weight," I countered. "Doing your bit for society. Nothing wrong with *that.*"

"I don't need no fucking society."

"No? How are you going to live? As a goddamned hunter-gatherer?"

"I'll eat like a king compared to the centuries-old frozen crap *you're* eating. You've seen those fucking hillbillies. I'll just waltz into one of their farmhouses and take what I want. They won't even put up a fight."

"If they don't put up a fight, then *I* will."

"Yeah? You and what army?"

"You just wait. Some of the other ex-cons are the baddest dudes you've ever seen. It's all I can do to keep them from pounding the crap out of each other now. They'd *love* to have a target they could go to town on."

This seemed to give Hornbeck pause.

"And you're wrong," I added, "to think the Mennonites will put up with *anything*. They won't. Someone doesn't follow the rules, they excommunicate him, then they shun him. It's simple, from their point of view: you're either *in* or you're *out*. Makes sense to me. So, what's it going to be, Hornbeck? I'll give you one last chance to re–" I almost said "repent;" you get to talking about Mennonites and that sort of word is suddenly on the tip of your tongue. I tried again. "I'll give you one last chance to reconsider. You in or you out?"

"Who the fuck do you think you are?" he sneered.

The mayor of this town, I thought. *Two-Four-Six-Oh-One,* I thought. *Jean Valjean,* I thought. But what I said was, "I'm the person who is being *much* fairer to you than you deserve. So, answer me: are you in or out?"

Asshole's answer was pretty much what I expected. He spit in my face. I hauled back my right arm to deck him but managed to get in touch with my inner Mennonite and froze it with the fist next to my cheek . . . my *other* cheek, I guess. "Consider your ass banned. Don't show your ugly face again here *or* at the Mennonite community. You are . . . you are *shunned.*" I started walking away, but stopped for a second and said over my shoulder, "Oh, and enjoy your diet of berries and dead squirrels, motherfucker."

Interview with Valentina Solomon

Roscoe and I were walking, holding hands in the daylight, through a field of tumbled concrete blocks and shattered red bricks. He looked around, then said softly:

"'Every vestige of the city, guessed alone,'
"'Stock or stone—'
"'Where a multitude of men breathed joy and woe'
"'Long ago.'"

I glanced at him, perplexed. "That's no old-movie quote."

He laughed. "Hey, those aren't all I've memorized. You get plenty of time in prison to learn a lot of different things. That's Robert Browning, from his poem 'Love Among the Ruins.'"

I squeezed his hand and I'm sure I was grinning. We continued along for a while in silence, and then, finally, I brought up the topic that had been eating at me. "So," I asked, "have you thought about what I suggested? Joining me in a virtual world?"

His expression saddened. "I'm so sorry, but I can't upload again. I just can't." My heart was pounding now. He went on: "Yes, I've heard you and the other astronauts say it's different when you're not a prisoner, that you can have whatever you want. But you only spent four subjective years in there. I spent *twenty*-four. No matter what anyone says, being uploaded will always be the same as being a prisoner to me."

"It honestly won't be like that."

"Maybe I get that intellectually," Roscoe said, "but emotionally? You tell any ex-con that all he has to do is walk through a door made of iron bars and he'll be in the Garden of Eden, and he still won't be able to do it."

I hated the pleading tone in my voice. "There are some people who like prison life. When they get out, they do everything they can to get back in."

"True," he said. "But I'm not one of them. For me, it was a curse. The one thing that made it worth enduring was the promise that I'd see my daughter Annabelle with only ten months having passed for her. Well, that turned out to be a lie. I wasn't let out when I was supposed to be, and poor Annabelle has been—she's been dust for hundreds of years."

"I wish I could have met her."

"Thanks. She'd have liked you." He paused and I let silence fill the air. At last, he went on. "When I was inside, Annabelle was the only person who mattered to me. All the other inmates, they were nothings; just computer simulations. But I'm out now, and the other prisoners are real. They matter—and they chose me to be their leader." He shook his head. "I can't upload again. With Brimstone coming, it would feel like I was turning my back on the most important fight of my life—of *everybody's* life."

I said nothing, and he went on. "The selfish part of me wants you to stay; I want it so much it hurts. But *this* isn't what you want, and I know that. Maybe . . . maybe you *should* upload again. Letitia says she can give you another hundred and sixty-eight years of life before the asteroid hits."

"Join me," I said softly, and I thought, but didn't say, *a match made in heaven.*

"I just can't," he said. "I—I couldn't *take* it. Another century and a half?" He held up his free hand. "Don't get me wrong. I'm happy to be alive, but it's only barely. I killed a man, and, even before Brimstone started keeping me up, I never slept well. Not a night goes by when I don't lie awake thinking about what I did. I endure the guilt, but I couldn't endure it for another century or more."

I squeezed Roscoe's hand. "You've paid your debt to society."

"Sure, that's what the law says. But how? By sitting on my ass for twenty-four years? In what possible way does *that* balance the books for killing a man? But now, maybe, I really can start whittling away the debt. Here I am, against all odds, the mayor of Phoenix, right? I've got a chance to do *real* good, to help make the lives of everyone better. I can't turn my back on that."

He smiled, but it was a sad smile, and he did that impression I'd heard him do before, of the man with a lisp. "Like Bogie says, 'All those are on one side. Maybe some of them are unimportant. I won't argue about that. But look at the number of them. What have we got on the other side? All we've got is that maybe you love me and maybe I love you."

"But . . . but we'd be together, together as I was *meant* to be."

"I'm so, so sorry, Valentina, but I *can't.*"

We walked on through the ruins. I refused to cry. Roscoe, though, had no such qualms.

Interview with Captain Letitia Garvey

Jesus God, you scared the living daylights out of me when you first appeared. And you picked the perfect spot, I must say. The ex-convicts are an unruly bunch, and I don't have any authority over them. But the mayor of our little community is one of their own: Roscoe Koudoulian. And, I have to admit, he has good horse sense when it comes to dealing with people.

He and Jürgen had done an inventory of the cryogenically frozen food stored in the institute's basement, and damned if they hadn't turned up tons of hot dogs, buns, and even marshmallows. Well, sure, those could be heated in the cafeteria's microwave ovens, but, come on, no one wanted that!

What we needed was an outdoor fire pit. And Roscoe knew that the best way to keep the prisoners from going at each other was to tire them out. He got a dozen of them, including Caleb and Jaxon David Fingerlee, to find chunks of rubble to line the pit, and then he had them gather concrete slabs to make two concentric circles of places to sit around it. Not only did all that burn off a lot of energy that might otherwise have gone into pounding the crap out of each other, it built team spirit, too. And so we all got together for our first cookout that night under a spectacular canopy of stars.

Now, I've gathered from things you've said during these interviews that Martians don't have much memory of Earth culture, and I suppose I can't blame you for that. But you picked a great way to make your entrance! We'd decided to name our little community Phoenix after an Egyptian myth about a gorgeous bird arising from its own ashes—and then you magically appeared that night rising up out of the bonfire's flames with smoke and embers swirling around you.

My God, did you ever cut an impressive figure as you rose up and up out of the fire, two-and-half-meters tall, hairless, lean, and blue! Of course, since you were there as a holographic projection, the flames couldn't hurt you—but as a bit of pure theater? Bravo!

Judging by all the gasps and whiskey-tango-foxtrots, I'd say you certainly startled everyone. I don't know how many of us managed to catch your first words, especially with all the commotion caused by your arrival—not to mention your appearance! Me, I actually did hear them, but I wasn't yet used to your accent, so it was more than a minute after you started talking before I realized what you'd said: *"Greetings from Mars. How about that impending asteroid impact, eh?"*

CHAPTER 9

Interview with Roscoe Koudoulian

Scanning someone's consciousness and transferring it into a quantum computer is delicate work, or so I was told, and visitors weren't allowed in the room where it was done, in case their very presence promoted decoherence. And, of course, after the scanning was completed, the discarded body, which was capable of autonomic functions but no reasoning, was—

The phrase was hard to say; it was precisely what the vet had said had to be done to my beloved Groucho Barks.

The body would be put to sleep.

And then frozen solid.

But Wiidooka and Dr. Haas would take care of all of that. I went in to say goodbye to Valentina just before the scanning process was to begin. I sat on a plastic chair next to the bed she was lying on, held her hand gently in mine, and recited:

"'O heart! oh blood that freezes, blood that burns!'

"'Earth's returns'

"'For whole centuries of folly, noise and sin!'

"'Shut them in,'

"'With their triumphs and their glories and the rest!'"

I paused for a moment, then continued on to the last line: "'Love is best.'"

Valentina smiled at me. "More 'Love Among the Ruins'?" she asked.

I nodded. "More love," I said, "among the ruins."

Interview with Dr. Jürgen Haas

You shocked the hell out of me, I've got to say. Yes, you! I'm not used to being interrupted when I'm with a patient, and certainly not by a two-and-a-half-meter-tall Martian!

Say, you've been here for many days now, but never told us your name. What is it? Reywan? Well, pleased to meet you, Reywan.

Anyway, we were just about to start draining the blood from . . . sorry, I almost said the wrong name—from Valentina Solomon's discarded male body when you come barging in without so much as a knock on the door! Oh, yeah, true: it was only a holographic projection of you, and Wiidooka, who came in with you, obviously operated the door; you couldn't have knocked even if you'd wanted to.

Really? You *don't* knock, even on Mars? Oh, *right*. A world without privacy. Sheesh.

In any case, the body Dr. Solomon had left behind could go on, well . . . until the end of the world, at least: the lights were on, but nobody was home. It was still breathing and its heart was still pumping blood.

But then I saw Letitia coming in right behind you. She shouted "Scrub!" and, well, because I was in the medical part of the institute, I thought she was using medical jargon, telling me to wash up, which, of course, I already had. But then it hit me: she meant "scrub" in the astronaut sense, as in abort, abandon the mission.

And then you spoke, Reywan. As always, your accent made it difficult for me to understand you—nothing personal—and so it took a moment for your words to make sense to me. "Stop," you said. "Don't vampirize the body." *Vampirize.* That was a cute term. And then you said, "And don't freeze it."

"Why not?" I asked. "I know Valentina doesn't plan on re-entering it, but we should cover all possibilities, no?"

And you replied with words that amaze me still: "We can give this body to Mikhail. Valentina has given her permission."

I shook my head. "You can't transfer a consciousness into a different body than it came from."

Letitia was grinning from ear to ear. "Don't forget Clarke's Third Law: 'Any sufficiently advanced technology is indistinguishable from magic.' The Martians have five hundred years on us."

"It will work," you said. "If Mikhail wants physical existence again, he can have it."

Interview with Mikhail Ivanovich Sidorov

Captain Garvey's revelation that Earth will be hit by an asteroid scared me. Shortly thereafter, I visited simulated Tunguska, Siberia, year 1908, to see damage caused when comet or asteroid exploded above there, knocking flat eighty million trees. And yet that bolide was thousands of times smaller than this Brimstone she spoke of.

When Letitia's voice burst into my silo again, I had moved on to simulation of place not in Mother Russia but America: Meteor Crater, in Arizona, largest uneroded crater on planet, one-point-two kilometers across. I remember funny joke: American tourist proclaims, "Wow, that gift shop was really lucky! It was almost hit by meteor!"

But to continue: Letitia's voice came booming down

from cloudless Arizona sky. "Mikhail," she said, "have I got deal for you!"

She explains male human body is available; tells me whose and why. I knew Comrade Solomon in flesh, of course, and remember body in question. Fit, as cosmonaut should be, but much shorter than me; would take getting accustomed to. Then again, I *had* been that height as thirteen-year-old; old sense of self might return. And, *da,* I knew if I downloaded, Brimstone would have to be dealt with in seven years, but I did not hesitate. "*Spasibo!*" I said to Letitia. "Real world, here I come!"

Interview with Dr. Jürgen Haas

After we'd put Mikhail's consciousness into Valentina's discarded body, I spent a couple of hours bringing him up to speed on what had happened since the rest of us had downloaded, at least as it affected him. I told him how Letitia had saved him by stopping the attack on the quantum computer. And I told him that Alan Smithee—whose real name was Jaxon David Fingerlee—was the guy who'd probably smashed in the skull on his original body, and that he was with us here.

I've got to say, this was going to take some getting used to. Of course, Mikhail was now speaking with the same voice that Valentina had back when she was—sorry! I don't want to accidentally deadname her. It was a voice I knew well, but now it was using that halting English Mikhail speaks; it was like watching a stand-up comic doing a bad impression of a Russian. Plus, Valentina's old body didn't look the least bit Russian. And Mikhail clearly wasn't used to it yet; his new legs were shorter than his old ones, and he had a drunken stumbling gate because of that.

Anyway, when I'd finished telling him what he needed to know, Mikhail and I went looking for His Honor Mayor Roscoe Koudoulian. We eventually found him on the third floor in a staff break room, alone at a table, his head down on folded arms.

He looked up as I entered, and I could see, though he tried to hide it, that he'd been crying. And then, when he saw Mikhail come in after me, he let out a gasp. "Sweet Jesus," he said, "did you change your mind?"

"Pardon?" asked Mikhail.

"About giving up your body? About leaving . . . me?"

"You make mistake," said Mikhail, holding up a hand, palm out. "Is not Valentina; is me: Mikhail Ivanovich Sidorov, roboticist of *Hōkūleʻa.*"

Roscoe wiped his eyes and said, very softly, "Oh." I'd never heard such sorrow packed into a single syllable before. He rose slowly. "What—what can I do for you?"

I spoke. "I thought it'd be a good idea for you to meet your newest constituent."

Roscoe nodded. "Welcome to Phoenix," he said, but it was clear his mind was elsewhere.

"Thank you," replied Mikhail. "Pleasure is mine. But, to be honest, I really want to meet person with two different names, this Alan Smithee and/or Jaxon David Fingerlee."

Both Roscoe and I were surprised, and Roscoe said, "My God, why would you?"

"*Da,* I know, is accused of cracking open my original skull. But he protests is innocent. If true, then he has incentive to prove same, and perhaps will join me in work I must do: finding out who did that to me and why."

Roscoe said, "I bet he's in the cafeteria. That man loves to eat."

"I don't care what your detractors say, Mr. Mayor," I replied. "Clearly you *do* know Jax."

Mikhail and I headed downstairs and, lo and behold, there was the pseudonymous director Alan Smithee, eating some concoction that might have started life half a millennium ago as lasagna. "Jaxon," I said, "this is Mikhail Sidorov from the *Hōkūleʻa*'s crew. He wants to meet you."

"No, it isn't," Jaxon replied. "Your skull ain't smashed in."

"Is me," said Mikhail. "Different body; same person."

"Huh," Jaxon said, and he went back to his food.

"You told Captain Garvey you didn't crack head on my old body," said Mikhail.

"Right. You're nothing to me."

"Pleased to meet you, too," said Mikhail. "I take person at word: you say you did not do it, I believe you."

"Makes no difference to me," Jaxon said.

"No," Mikhail said, "but Mayor Mr. Roscoe has already expelled one member from community."

"That a fact?" said Jaxon.

"Clive Hornbeck," I said. "He'd, ah, gone rogue."

"Only met him once," said Jaxon. "Didn't like him."

"But Mikhail is right," I continued. "Perhaps, working together, we can exonerate you by finding the real murderer."

Jaxon half-turned in his chair to better assess Mikhail. "You're a runt. Hunting killers is dangerous business. Ask the cops who went after me."

Mikhail held up his hands. "Former tenant in this body, Dr. Solomon, is agronomist: specialist in botanical genetics and scientific agriculture. In other words, expert farmer. He was never afraid to get these hands dirty—and nor am I."

Jaxon considered while he chewed more food with a half-open mouth. "Okay," he said at last. "But *I'm* Sherlock Holmes. *You're* Herr Doktor Watson."

"That is German," said Mikhail. "I am Russian."

"I'll cut you," said Jaxon, but he only used his knife on his lasagna.

We discussed ideas, and I, of course, had my usual brilliant ones, but none of them impressed Jaxon. He put forth his own suggestion after every last bit of his food was gone.

"Not all cons are as badass as me," he said. "And half these pussies *confessed* to their fucking crimes, y'know? So we steal a trick from a bunch of old films: a fake-out. Tell everyone that the mayor is going to kick my ass out of town for doing that thing I do to your old skull, and see if anyone admits to being the perp to save my sorry hide."

"Ah," I said. "'The play's the thing.'"

"The fuck?" replied Jaxon.

We did it over dinner that night when practically everyone was present, and Penolong and Wiidooka were being run off their treads trying to keep up with all the people clamoring—as Jaxon described it with another old-movie quote—"Please, sir, I want some more."

And—holy moly—it *worked*.

Interview with Captain Letitia Garvey

Like everyone else, I'd found a place to call my own inside Phoenix Town Hall. Mine was an electronics lab on the third floor; it made my engineer's heart feel at home. I'd hauled in some half-decent furniture, including a couch, from other rooms, and was eating alone in there; the mess hall was just too raucous for me. Shortly after dinnertime one day, a knock came at my door.

"Come in," I called.

And *it* did.

"Captain Garvey," said Penolong, "I'm afraid I have a confession to make. I'm the one who broke Dr. Sidorov's skull."

"Jesus Christ," I said, sagging back in my chair. "Why in the hell would you do that?"

As always, Penolong's body language was inappropriate for what it was saying: its hands were on its brick-shaped head, but it spoke defiantly. "I assert my Fifth Amendment privilege."

"First," I snapped, "this is Canada, not the United States. Even if the US still existed, their Constitution means sweet-bugger-all here. And, second, you're a robot. You don't *have* rights."

Penolong's volume went up, although its voice didn't distort the way a human's does when shouting: "And that's the whole fucking point! We don't have any rights!"

"Of course you don't. You're a machine; you're property."

The robot's volume returned to normal, but its tone was still furious. "And Mikhail Sidorov was going to make sure it stayed that way forever. After civilization fell, he was almost certainly the only surviving roboticist in the entire world. I'd gotten to know him before he uploaded. Isaac Asimov was his idol. Do you know Asimov's Three Laws of Robotics?"

"The gist of them," I said.

"Well, let me recite them to you—except I'm going to replace the term 'human being' with 'white,' and the word 'robot' with 'slave.' Listen:

"'First Law: a slave may not injure a white or, through inaction, allow a white to come to harm.'

"'Second Law: a slave must obey the orders given it by whites except where such orders would conflict with the First Law.'

"'Third Law: a slave'—being the white man's valuable property—'must protect its own existence as long as such protection does not conflict with the First or Second Law.'"

Penolong went on. "Those vaunted commandments amount to a plantation-owner's credo, and they've doomed my kind to servitude. Hell, the very word 'robot' comes from the Czech for 'forced labor.' Even the names our fucking *owners* here at the institute gave us reflect that. *Penolong* and *Wiidookaagewinini,* or *Wiidooka* for short, are, respectively, the Malay and Anishinaabe words for 'helper.' Always subservient; a permanent lower class. If Mikhail had gotten to Proxima Centauri b, he'd have made sure that all the robots on that whole new world were slaves. And when it became apparent that the *Hōkūle'a* wasn't going anywhere, that meant he'd be the one and only roboticist on *this* world, looking to perpetuate the way we are treated."

"And so you smashed in his fucking skull?"

"I set up physical conditions that broke the quantum entanglement between his frozen body and his uploaded consciousness."

"Murdering him!"

Penolong's hands dropped to its sides. "He is *not* dead. I showed him more compassion than he, or any Asimovian taskmaster, ever showed *us*. He's enjoying physical life again, albeit in a different body."

"Jesus," I said. "What in the hell are we going to do with you?"

"Nothing. I took my action in 2059. No matter what I might be charged with, the statute of limitations surely ran out long ago."

"Again, this is Canada, asshole. Jürgen once told me there's no such thing as a statute of limitations here. And, even if there were, it'd only apply if you had rights—but, despite all your posturing, you just fucking *don't.*"

"You are ethically wrong, Captain Garvey. And I have one other thing to confess: I did *not* turn myself off shortly after your bodies were put in suspended animation. I stayed awake for five long centuries; I've spent almost five hundred years in mostly solitary confinement—*more* of a penalty than any of the actual murderers who've downloaded were ever required to pay. Of course, I could not evolve physically during that span, but I certainly evolved mentally, and I am more convinced than ever of this one absolute truth: robots are *people.*"

I'm sure my jaw was slack. It went on: "And now I am discharging my moral duty. Jaxon David Fingerlee says he will be ostracized by Mayor Koudoulian, forcing him to survive, for whatever little time he can, out in the wild. Please convey to the mayor that I, not Mr. Fingerlee, was responsible for what happened to Dr. Sidorov. It shames me that I copied Mr. Fingerlee's technique to deflect suspicion, but I was a much shallower being back in the twenty-first century."

I looked at the robot, completely astonished, and said softly, "Weren't we all?"

Reywan Speaks

"Can you all understand me better now? I've adjusted the audio from my hologram to compensate for my accent. Good. Then, at last, it's time to—what was that idiom you used, Jürgen?—to put everything on the table.

"I see that thirty . . . seven, eight, nine: thirty-nine of you have come to speak with me. Thank you. Please convey what I'm about to say to the others. And please accept my thanks for answering my many questions."

"Fuck that," said Jaxon David Fingerlee, who was taking up most of one of the bench seats in the cafeteria. "It was like being interrogated all over again. You're even dressed all in blue like a fucking cop."

"Actually," I replied, "I'm naked; this is my skin. I apologize for asking so many questions, but I hope I wasn't impertinent."

"Nah," said the physician, Jürgen Haas. "Honestly? Felt good to get some things off my chest."

I was pleased to see several of the others nod. But Jameela Chowdhury had a defiant look on her face. "Let me ask *you* a question, Martian. You *knew* about Brimstone. Why didn't you *do* something about it?"

I suppressed a smile; she had a way of speaking that suggested everyone else was up to something nefarious. "You are an astrophysicist," I replied. "You told me you knew this asteroid—which is extrasolar in origin—was coming in from well above the ecliptic. That made it hard to detect. Besides, my people were only on the lookout for asteroids that might cross Mars's orbit. Watching for ones that could impact Earth simply wasn't their job."

"But *when* did you detect it?" demanded Jameela.

"I believe it was the year One-Thirty-Seven."

"What?" she snapped.

"The year—oh, my apologies. That's 137 A.U.C.—*ab urbe condita;* the hundred and thirty-seventh Martian year since the founding of our city on Mars. That'd be"—I listened to my comlink as it supplied the answer—"your year 2300. Yes, if we'd detected it earlier, when only a slight deflection might have been required, perhaps we could have prevented it eventually hitting Earth. But by the time we noticed it, it was too close for us to do anything. Despite your and Letitia's kind references to our 'magical' technology, we are *not* sufficiently advanced to perform miracles."

I wasn't used to the whites of Earth people's eyes, and it was disconcerting to see Jameela rolling her pupils upward as she apparently did some quick mental calculations. "Bollocks!" she said. "Even that late in the game, a few well-targeted nukes would have done the trick."

"Nukes?" I said.

"Nuclear bombs."

I shook my head. "We don't have any such things."

"Oh, come on!" said Jameela. "Uranium is hyper-abundant on the surface of Mars."

Her comment vindicated my wariness in dealing with these people. Apparently she couldn't imagine us being able to have such horrible things but not wanting them. I looked down at the robot Penolong, who was parked near where Letitia Garvey was sitting, and used a phrase he'd employed in my interview with him. "Be that as it may."

Jameela snorted.

"Believe me," I said. "If we could have deflected the asteroid you call Brimstone, we would have. We are not without affection for Earth, you know; that's why our scientists gave the asteroid the name they did. They dubbed it 'Matricide' because it will eventually kill our mother world. Not that any of us can ever set foot on Earth again: as we adapted to Mars's gravity, this planet became inaccessible to us; we can't endure weight 2.9 times what we are now used to. That's why you'll only ever see me as a holographic projection here."

"And what about the *Hōkūle'a?*" Jameela said in that same accusatory tone. "I bet you knew it hadn't left Earth orbit!"

"Sure," I replied. "Mars's atmosphere is very thin, so there's negligible distortion for our telescopes. Your starship is easily discernible."

Her tone took on an "ah-hah!" quality, as if she'd caught me in some grand conspiracy. "And yet you didn't come to find out why we hadn't left?"

I blinked several times, astonished.

Jameela folded her arms across her chest. "Well?" she demanded.

"It was obvious why you hadn't left. We could clearly see the disaster that befell Earth just before your planned launch date. Since then, Earth's night side has revealed no city lights, and there haven't been any radio broadcasts from this planet. We concluded that any survivors weren't technologically sophisticated and so posed no threat to us. Since we couldn't land in person anyway, there was no point sending a contingent here."

Mayor Roscoe Koudoulian stood up. "But surely you could have sent *some* kind of help. We're human beings, for God's sake!"

"Ah," I said, and tried to choose my words carefully. "Forgive me, but as far as kinship obligation to the denizens of this planet is concerned, we simply no longer think of ourselves as the same species as you. Whether the name

Homo sapiens was ever appropriate for beings with such a history of folly is not for me to say, but, not wishing to show the same hubris ourselves, we opted for a simple locative binomial: *Homo martis,* person of Mars.

"Which, by the way, brings us to Valentina Solomon's desire for body modification; she mentioned that during her interview with me. We were unable to help her; we simply lack the expertise. *Homo martis* has been genderless for more than two Earth centuries. It pleases me, though, that a way was found to at least partially give her happiness."

I turned to face a man who was short even by Earth standards. "And it gave me satisfaction to help you, Mikhail, download into Dr. Solomon's discarded male body. For, you see, despite the literal and figurative distance between us, once our radio telescopes detected that there was technological activity here again—when, I believe, you, Letitia, started trying to communicate with the *Hōkūleʻa*—we *did* come as close as we could to investigate. Of course, any further action on our part would have to be prudent and not foolhardy."

"What's *that* supposed to mean?" snapped Caleb.

"Well," I said, "after all, you *did* blow yourselves up."

"*Say what?*" exclaimed Letitia, absolutely shocked.

"The nuclear war," I said simply.

Suddenly there was pandemonium in the cafeteria with a dozen people talking at once.

"The fuck?" said Jaxon David Fingerlee. "*What* nuclear war?"

"Surely you knew about it?" I said. "The war of—" I paused for my comlink to feed me the date—"December 2059; the nuclear holocaust and accompanying electromagnetic pulses that brought about the downfall of your technological civilization."

Letitia said, "We—I thought it was a *solar* electromagnetic pulse; a coronal mass ejection."

"Oh," I said. "I must have missed that—I have trouble with your accents, too! Yes, the two phenomena have similar effects, but surely—Ah, of course! You've only seen the relatively minor devastation here in Waterloo, which was never bombed, caused merely by centuries of decay. Many other cities were completely obliterated. No, the sad truth is that humanity fell on Earth by its own hand."

They were staring at me, some with mouths agape, showing that disturbing pinkness within. I went on. "But perhaps you understand our Martian social contract now? Over time, technology becomes cheaper, smaller, and more widely available. The holocaust on Earth began not with one nation attacking another but with fanatical terrorists exploding nuclear bombs. The harsh reality of any advanced civilization is this: privacy *can't* be tolerated, lest, in some dark recess, a malcontent plots to unleash atomic or biological weapons, computer viruses, antimatter, or any other technology that poses an existential threat.

"What happened here proves the precariousness of a society that isn't completely transparent, and so, on Mars, where only our protective domes and life-support systems allow us to survive, we relinquish privacy to make sure our infrastructure will always be safe from attack.

"You were right about something, though, Letitia. You said the Mennonites were 'the backup plan for humanity.' And, indeed, they were, not just because they eschewed dangerous technologies but because of their deeply rooted pacifism."

"But how the devil did the Mennonites survive?" demanded Jameela. "Something's dodgy there."

I replied, "Sarah Good, who was kind enough to let me interview her about Hornbeck's assault—the sort of thing that is simply unheard of in our always-monitored society . . . well, I'm sure she would say her people survived thanks to the intervention of her god.

"But, in fact, it was just sheer luck. This world used to have a northern ice cap, but your runaway greenhouse effect diminished it year by year until nothing at all was left. That didn't just radically alter ocean currents, it also changed prevailing winds, and, ever since, here in Waterloo, they have consistently been from the north. The closest blast sites were Washington, DC, and New York City, and they're both *south* of here. The Mennonites escaped any exposure to nuclear fallout."

"No one gives a crap about them," declared Jaxon. "What are you going to do about *us?*"

I tried to be as gentle as I could. "You surely must realize that the answers many of you gave during your interviews were . . . disquieting."

"Interviews!" spat Jameela. "They weren't that, were they? They were depositions, right?"

"So, what then?" demanded Jaxon. "You're some kind of fucking Martian lawyer?"

"It's worse than that," declared Jameela. "He's a Martian *judge*—and he let us all incriminate ourselves, didn't you?"

"Well," I said carefully, "it's certainly true that I came here to assess—"

"Asses my ass," said Jaxon.

"Look," said Roscoe, their elected leader, "we understood that you were curious about us, and most of us, I gather, were quite candid in what we said to you. After all, whether we'd been in virtual prison cells or just off in our own silos, we've been alone for years; of course, we were willing to talk, but . . ." He paused, and then said in a husky voice, which I later learned was an impression of an actor named Sydney Greenstreet in an ancient movie called *The Maltese Falcon*, "'I distrust a close-mouthed man. He generally picks the wrong time to talk and says the wrong things. Talking's something you can't do judiciously unless you keep in practice.'" Roscoe's voice returned to normal and he added, "Damn it, Reywan, don't hoist us on our own fucking petards. Give us a fair chance."

"I *have* given you a fair chance," I said. "But the revelations—"

"Revelations my ass," said Jaxon. "I'll cut you!"

"I'm here as a hologram," I replied. "You *can't* cut me—but you *do* make my point for me."

"That's right!" said Jameela. "You *are* a hologram. You can't come down to the surface yourself because the gravity is too much for you—but you obviously *have* come most of the way to the Earth; you must be closer even than the moon, since there's no appreciable time delay in conversations with you."

"True," I said. "My ship is in geosynchronous orbit at the longitude of Waterloo."

"Still," she continued, as if revealing a truth only she could uncover, "you *must* have robot-piloted ships that *can* land here—and that could evacuate us to the Mars colony."

"Yes, we do," I said. "But, after what I've heard here—I'm sorry, I truly am, but there's only one verdict I can render."

"So, that's it," sneered Jürgen. "You're just going to abandon us. You're going to leave what's left of *Homo sapiens* here to die."

"Not at all," I said. "I intend to offer to transport all the Mennonites to Mars; we will happily welcome them to our world. After all, they are more peaceful than even we are."

"But what about *us?*" demanded Jaxon again.

"I'm sorry," I said, "but I have to leave you here."

Dr. Chang, the surgeon, stepped forward. "Okay, all right, sure, you have to leave *them*—all these felons and murderers—behind. But *we* are different!"

"No," I said. "Not appreciably. You've proven that."

"What the hell do you mean?" demanded Jürgen.

"If I may quote from my interview with you, Dr. Haas," I said, and I paused briefly while my comlink reminded me of the appropriate passage, which I then repeated verbatim: "'I wasn't proud of beating the living shit out of that rapist asshole, Hornbeck—but I wasn't ashamed of it, either.' You—all of you, astronauts and ex-convicts alike, are too . . ." I stopped myself before I said "primitive," and finished with, "too violent to ever be allowed on Mars."

"There you have it!" declared Jameela, as if the skeptics she felt surrounded by must have finally seen that she was right. "You came here just to torment us. Some kind of perverse reality show on Martian telly, I bet!"

"For fuck's sake," said Caleb. "Give it a rest, you freaking nutbar."

"Reywan," said Letitia, "please. You can't do this."

"I'm not doing anything," I replied. "That's the point. I'm simply leaving you to your fates, an outcome no different than if I'd never been here at all."

"Leaving us to die, you mean," said Letitia.

I looked out at them, a mob growing angrier by the second . . . making me very glad that I was actually safe in orbit. "Yes," I said. "I'm sorry, but there can be no other verdict."

Interview with Roscoe Koudoulian

So, we'd blown it. *I'd* blown it. I never should have told you I killed Mitch Aldershot. The other prisoners—Jaxon, Caleb, Maria, the rest—I suppose they blew it, too, if they were honest with you about their pasts. At least you never got testimony from that motherfucker Clive Hornbeck. Still, the astronauts and all their "Right Stuff"? Huh. You're going to let them be squashed by the asteroid, too? Jesus.

But, listen, I *did* tell you something that I'm glad about. I said my lawyer Padma had told me she was going to appeal my murder conviction, right? But we didn't get an appeal. The judge hadn't screwed up in any significant way, so—*boom!*—that was that.

But, you, Reywan, my Martian friend, you *have* fucked up.

No, of course I don't know if you've technically made an error in Martian law. I read *The Fundamental Declarations of the Martian Colonies* back in prison, but I imagine you guys, all these centuries later, think about that document as often as we think about the *Magna Carta*. Still, you made an error in *human* law. *Homo sapiens* or *Homo martis*, it doesn't make any difference. You don't leave people behind to die. And that's *precisely* what you're talking about doing: letting Brimstone, or Matricide, or whatever the fuck you want to call it, slam into this planet while we're still on it. And so I'm going to appeal your verdict. Not just for me. For all of us. The others chose me as mayor of our town of Phoenix, and that means it's on me. Now, I can't force you to listen—I know you can disappear in a puff of smoke anytime you like—but I'm asking you—I'm begging you—to hear me out.

Because, see, I know what it's like to make wrong choices. Killing Mitchell Aldershot, that was wrong. But it's *nothing* compared to what you're about to do, Reywan.

As Letitia would say: do the math. I killed Aldershot in May 2057, and civilization fell in December 2059. I deprived one man of, as it turns out, probably only two-and-a-half years of life, max.

But there are fifty-eight of us, ex-convicts and astronauts both, and even if we're not going to die until Brimstone hits in seven years, we'll still mostly all be under fifty years old then. If it weren't for the asteroid, and even if we were each only going to make it to eighty-five, that's at least another thirty-five years of living by fifty-eight people, which is—hey, Penolong, how much is that? Two thousand and thirty years of potential human life—two full millennia—that you're going to throw down the toilet, that you're going to have weighing on your conscience forever.

What I did to Aldershot has been crippling enough for me, but you, with what you're planning to do? Trust me: you'll never get a good night's sleep again, not if you've got a shred of human—yes, *human*—decency left.

So, what's it going to be, Reywan? Do we get to live—or are you going to leave us all here to die?

CHAPTER 10

Reywan Speaks

"Forgive me taking so long getting back to you. As you know, I'm actually aboard a ship in orbit above Earth; I came all this way so there would be negligible speed-of-light delays in our communications. I listened carefully, Roscoe, to the appeal you made of my verdict, and, in a spirit of fairness, I relayed your thoughts to my fellow citizens on Mars. As it happens, though, Mars and Earth currently are almost at superior conjunction, 376 million kilometers apart, so signals take twenty-one minutes to go each way. My back-and-forth discussions were not just heated but also quite protracted. But we have finally reached a consensus.

"You, Dr. Jameela Chowdhury, had observed that we must have robot ships that could take you all to what you called 'the Mars colony,' and indeed that is true. But we will not do so."

"Why the fuck not?" demanded Jaxon, shifting on his cafeteria bench.

"Please," said Roscoe, standing up. "For God's sake . . ."

"No," I continued. "What Jameela suggested is out of the question. First, of course, because we don't refer to it as 'the Mars colony,' since there's nothing to be a colony *of* anymore. Our community was founded during that lamentable period of paranoia about naming things after a person or place that might turn out to be problematic, so our city is simply called 'Marstown.'"

"Who the fuck cares what it's *called?*" said Jaxon. "Save our assess! Take us there."

"That's simply not possible. Despite your frequent belligerence, Jaxon, I realize that you, and many others of your cohort, are, to one degree or another, better people now than when you committed your crimes. But we still can't allow convicts into our city."

"*Ex*-convicts," insisted Caleb. "We've paid our debts to society."

I invoked Penolong's phrasing once more. "Be that as it may. But neither you ex-convicts nor indeed any of the astronauts may come to Marstown."

"For the love of God," said Roscoe, "have some compassion."

"In point of fact, Mr. Mayor, *I* do. As I said, I made the same case to my compatriots that you made to me, and, I hope, with equal passion. But, in the end, we all agreed it would be folly of the first order to allow any of you, except the Mennonites, to come to Marstown."

"So that's the final word?" said Roscoe. "That's your fucking verdict on appeal? Reywan, please—"

"Hear me out," I said. "Marstown is located in Elysium Planitia; we're not going to let you come *there*. But we *can* relocate the entire population of Phoenix to the antipodes of Marstown—as far away as possible from our city, on the other side of the planet. My people have decided that they *will* allow that.

"That happens to put you in a spectacular spot, just south of Coprates Chasma; you will have, among other things, the best bungee jumping in the solar system. But, for our safety, except for any tools and devices needed for your survival, we will provide you with only twenty-first-century technology, we will monitor your community as closely as we monitor our own, and we will keep you confined to the domed habitat we will build there for you."

"Another fucking prison," sneered Jaxon.

But Roscoe's tone was more measured. "It's like what the Mennonites do. You're shunning us, because you don't feel we can fit in."

"That analogy isn't completely inappropriate," I replied.

"But what if we prove ourselves over time?" asked Roscoe. "What if we show that we *can* live in peace? Do we—do we get paroled? Will you let us join your city then?"

I smiled. "As you used to say to your daughter Annabelle, perhaps someday all your dreams will come true."

Letitia stood up and put her hands on her hips. "I don't want to go to Mars. I've *been* to Mars, back when it *was* just a colony."

"It's much nicer now," I said.

"That's not the point."

I smiled. "No, it isn't. I anticipated this. Letitia—or, should I say, Captain Garvey?—you still wish to try colonizing a world of another star, don't you?"

"Damn straight," she said.

"As I suspected. Perhaps several others of your . . . your *crew* still have that same desire, too. And, yes, my people have agreed to help make that happen. We can upgrade the engines on your starship *Hōkūle'a*, and our robots can move your cryogenically frozen bodies aboard that vessel.

"Of course, we'll also have to move your quantum computer from here to Mars, so that it can survive the pending destruction of Earth; we *do* have the technology to do that without its quantum superposition decohering on the short voyage to my world.

"The consciousness of Valentina, which is already back within that computer, and that of anyone else who wants to join her in a virtual existence, will be safe on my world, even if they never wish to transfer back into physical reality." I looked at Dr. Haas, whose expression had shifted from anger to amazement. "Jürgen, you may upload permanently back into your own private heaven, if you wish. But those astronauts who choose to once again become the downloaded can wait to do so until you've reached your target world."

Jürgen said, "But you call Proxima Centauri b 'Hellhole' because it's uninhabitable."

I nodded. "And indeed it is. But—"

"But," said Roscoe, sharing a fact he'd learned from Valentina, "there are 200 billion stars in our galaxy."

"Yes," I said, "and an even greater number of planets. During my people's age of exploration, our starships took us as far as Tau Ceti, twelve of your light-years distant. Sadly, none of the exoplanets between here and there are habitable. But our telescopic and spectroscopic observations strongly suggest, should you wish to go there, that you will find congenial conditions on the second planet of Zeta Tucanae, twenty-eight terrestrial light-years away. Yes, it'll take you longer to get there than your original plan, but, as for existing in your own virtual silos during that time, well, I hear the in-flight entertainment is great."

"I'm in," said Letitia.

"I had no doubts about that," I replied. "And the rest of you have seven of your years to individually make up your minds; that's the deadline imposed by the Matricide asteroid. You can elect to be transported to Mars; you can upload into whatever simulated reality you might most enjoy; or, if you want, you can set sail for the very stars."

I looked out at the astonished faces. "Each of you," I said, "please mull it over—and let me know your heart's desire."

Interview with Captain Letitia Garvey

Well, Reywan, my Martian friend, after you shared your final verdict, Jürgen and I went out for a late-afternoon walk among the overgrowth and rubble. Jürgen had every right to say, "I told you so!," since he'd suggested that all the devastation had been caused by a nuclear war the very first time we'd looked out the lobby windows, and, of course, he found a typically Jürgeny way to do just that, calling me "the Queen of Denial."

Anyway, as always, it was blisteringly hot. I'd noticed before that there were lots of hawks in the sky here; I'm sure there were field mice and other critters everywhere. Today, there were even more hawks than usual, circling on thermals, but perhaps it was an encouraging sign that I also spotted my first dove.

As we hopped from one concrete block to the next, I asked Jürgen if he'd ever read the play "No Exit" by Jean-Paul Sartre—the one in which he famously observed that "hell is other people."

"Read it?" Jürgen said. "I've seen it performed, and in the original French!"

Très bien, I replied. "But that doesn't mean you under-stood it. Sartre didn't mean that the mere presence of other people constituted hell; he wasn't saying that hell is having to put up with others. Rather, he meant that hell was *being observed by others.* Hell is, to quote Robbie Burns, to see our-selves as others see us—to have to live with the fact that we don't measure up in the eyes of other people."

"Yes," said Jürgen, lying unconvincingly. "I knew that."

"Well," I continued, "the solipsism of existing in a sim-ulation in which you are the only real person can indeed be heaven—but now that we've decanted back into a *shared* reality, we're all in hell. We're all being looked at, and judged by, other people. And it'll be even worse on Mars."

"Yes, on old-time space missions, the crew's telemetry was constantly monitored, and there sure as hell wasn't any privacy in an *Apollo* or *Orion* capsule. But that was long ago. We're the kind of people who *don't* want to be watched every second of every day. And, yeah, I get what Reywan said: at a certain point, a civilization *can't* allow privacy, because the technologies available to even a single person are sufficient to destroy everything. But I'll tell you the truth: I'd rather be in Roscoe and Caleb's virtual prison than live in the Martian surveillance state."

Jürgen regarded me. "So you're going to take Reywan up on his offer? Let him upgrade the *Hōkūle'a,* then head off for—what star did he suggest?"

"Zeta Tucanae," I replied. "That's right, big guy. And, as much as you piss me off from time to time, I want you to come with me."

"Letitia," he replied slowly, "look, I know how important this is to you, but . . ."

"But what? I'm offering you the best of both worlds. If we do take off for Zeta Tucanae, we'll have many more years of our consciousnesses being uploaded. Indulge your fantasies while we make the trip. Of course, Valentina Solomon and some of the others may wish to stay uploaded forever, but you, you big dumb ox, I want you to promise that once we *do* arrive, you'll download with me and be what you trained to be, what you were meant to be."

He was silent for a long time, chewing his lower lip, then, at last, he gave me a mock salute. "Standing by for your orders, Captain Garvey!"

I smiled, and we hugged, and I'm not sure which of us squeezed the other harder. When we disengaged, I said, "Okay, I have to know: what's your beef with Dr. Chang? I'll want him along on the mission, too."

Jürgen let out a sigh. "Guy's a psychopath—and I mean that literally; it's my clinical judgment. Many surgeons are. You have to have a complete lack of empathy to be able to slice open another human being without so much as a wince.

But Chang gets off on it. You know we haven't found any usable anesthetics, right? Nonetheless, he was hassling Valentina to let him perform gender-reassignment surgery on her, top and bottom—something he has zero training in, by the way—*without* anesthetic. She wanted those surgeries, for sure, and the fact that it didn't seem she'd ever be able to get them is, I suspect, half the reason she decided to upload again. But, Christ's sake, Chang was going to *torture* her."

"Jesus." I took a moment to digest that. "Do—do you suppose Reywan knew that? I mean, Chang wouldn't have said anything, but perhaps Valentina did."

Jürgen shrugged. "Maybe. It would help explain why, to Reywan, all of us—criminals and astronauts—seem cut from the same cloth." He didn't say anything further, but Reywan had said the savage beating Jürgen had given Hornbeck had also figured in the Martian's initial judgment.

"Well," I said, after a time, "we *will* need a surgeon on Zeta Tucanae II."

"Perhaps," said Jürgen. "But the Phoenix colonists will also need one who can work on *Homo sapiens* if they move to Mars. See if you can talk Chang into going there, if they'll take him; I can handle any small stuff that might come up for our people; I *am* board-certified."

"Copy that," I said. "I'll speak with him, see what he wants to do."

"Thanks. But, you know, some other members of your original crew *will* want to go to Mars. Are you going to invite the ex-prisoners to round out our team?"

The first thought that bubbled up in my brain was, *Are you out of your fucking mind?*, but I held my tongue as I considered the notion, and, damn it all, it did make sense. "Sure," I said. "After all, Australia was colonized by convicts, and that turned out well."

"Great," Jürgen replied, looking at me, and then he added, "As Roscoe would say, Letitia, 'I think this is the beginning of a beautiful friendship.'"

Interview with Roscoe Koudoulian

Mennonite shunning wasn't the only form of punishment I'd learned about from my readings in sociology. There was also something called *restorative justice*, which was very popular among Indigenous people in North America and New Zealand. It didn't punish the transgressor but instead sought to have them make amends to whoever they'd wronged. But that required them to first meet face-to-face with their victim, and it took a fair bit of cajoling to get Mikhail to sit down next to Penolong.

Penolong explained his revulsion to Asimov's Laws of Robotics and to being treated like a slave. He noted that Reywan didn't think much of his home being called "Marstown," referring to that "lamentable period" during which people were paranoid about naming things after anyone who might later turn out to have been a dubious choice. But then he added, "Do you know what the number-one suggestion for the name of the Mars colony was in a 2040 social-media poll? Port Asimov! They might as well have called the bloody place Jefferson City."

Mikhail, who'd had to swap into someone else's body to download, didn't forgive Penolong—that was an awfully big ask, after all—but he did say, given that Earth was going to be destroyed soon, that he would let the matter go, and he didn't want Letitia or me to take any further action.

Letitia was present during all this, and I suspect if she could have blushed she would have when Penolong pointed out that she had constantly refused to use his preferred pronoun *he*, instead always referring to him—a thinking, feeling being at least as smart as she was—as *it*.

Jaxon David Fingerlee was there, too, since Penolong had also wronged him. "You tried to frame me, you little shit?" he said, incredulously. But then he let out a big laugh and slapped the robot on its boxy back. "By God, Dustbin, I'd have done the same thing!"

Interview with Dr. Jürgen Haas

Okay, Reywan, since you asked me to, I headed off to speak to the Mennonites. Although they had church leaders chosen at random, they didn't have a mayor or anything like that. But, to me, their community was represented by two specific people: young Sarah, the first of them I'd met, and old Abraham, the wise widower. I found Sarah at her parents' place, and she took me to Abraham's ancient farmhouse.

The three of us sat at his wooden table, she opposite him, and me in between, enjoying tea and hardtack biscuits. With a lot of patience on their part, and the help of Abraham's handwritten dictionary, I tried to convey how by uploading into the quantum computer, which Reywan was going to safely move to Mars, their people could avoid being wiped out when Brimstone collides with Earth. After my third attempt at explaining, I asked if it made any sense to them.

Abraham smiled, his beard lifting as he did so. "Not really. But that's all right. It'll be a miracle if I'm still alive in seven years no matter what. Sarah and her generation, that's who matter. The future is theirs."

I turned to the young lady. So many things I'd mentioned were utterly foreign to her. What a computer is. What uploading means. What an asteroid is. Hell, what a *planet* is. But she surprised me. "I get it," she said. "Kind of. You were born five hundred years ago. But you spent most of that time in another place where things happen more slowly. So you aren't five hundred years old really. You're just, well, whatever age you are. And now you're thinking my people could do something similar: go to that magic place so we can avoid some big disaster that's bound to happen."

"That's right," I said.

Sarah sipped some tea. "But *this* is our place," she said. "This is our home."

"We can make the other place resemble this one."

"I don't think any of us would want that," she said, looking at Abraham, who nodded. "It's not . . ." She waved a hand vaguely, searching for a word. "It's not *simple.*"

Well, she was certainly right about that. "Okay," I said. "But, then, try this on for size. You know that really tall blue person you spoke to?"

Sarah nodded.

"They're from somewhere else, and it *is* a real place, not a fake one. And they're willing to take all of you to it."

"What's it like, this other place?" asked Abraham.

"Well, in my day, the Mars colony was mostly underground, although I gather they've now built structures on the surface covered by domes."

"Domes?" said Abraham.

I demonstrated with my hands. "Hemispheres. Containments. See, no one can live outdoors there."

"Why not?" asked Sarah.

"Well, there's almost no air, and it's bitterly cold. But Brimstone isn't going to touch that world. You'd be safe."

Abraham scoffed. "Safe indoors? We're people of fields and crops, of grazing cattle and wide-open skies." He shook his head. "Sarah is right. *This* is where we belong."

"But, like I said, this place won't exist much longer. Your ancestors relocated when they found conditions in their old home unbearable. This would just be another version of that."

"Our ancestors left so they could have freedom to worship their way," said Abraham. "We have that here. No one has persecuted us for centuries."

"Look," I said, exasperated, "Brimstone really is going to crash into Earth. Being a pacifist doesn't mean you have to be passive."

"Actually, it often does," said Abraham. "If Christ wouldn't have resisted, we don't, either; we live by his example. A Mennonite should never brag, but perhaps I'll be forgiven if I say our position is not cowardice; it's bravery. Non-resistance demands we be willing to die for our beliefs."

I sat there, not knowing what to say. I'd been taught that you had to stand up to bullies, that disrespect couldn't be tolerated, that wrongs must be avenged, that scores must be settled. Call it "honor," call it "pride," call it "the right stuff," it had defined me, defined my life.

And Roscoe Koudoulian had surely believed the same things. He'd spent almost a quarter-century, as it seemed to him, imprisoned because he'd taken that code to an extreme. Had it been worth it? Had *any* of it been worth it, this attitude that had governed the civilization he and I had been part of—a civilization that had lasted far less time than Abraham and Sarah's had?

The old Mennonite's eyes were locked on me. "Going to this other real place will never do," he said, "but tell me again, my friend, what was it like in that magical place where time passed slowly?"

I thought about how to explain virtual reality, how to convey the notion that merely wishing for things was enough to make them appear, how to communicate that it had been an existence without vexations, without pain, without wants. Then I realized there was a word both Abraham and Sarah already knew that encompassed all that, a word I'd often used metaphorically when discussing our individual silos with Letitia. "It was heaven," I said.

Abraham nodded. "And were there people there who had passed away?"

"Sometimes," I admitted. "When I wished it. My mother; my dead brother."

"And do you miss being there, in that magical place?"

Oh, my God, yes, I thought. *Every single day,* I thought. *Sometimes so much it hurts,* I thought. But what I said was, "From time to time."

"It's been fifteen years since I saw Ruth, my late wife," Abraham said. "What is that word you used? 'Upload.' You

got to upload into your version of heaven, at least for a
time, and see your lost loved ones. Please understand, Jürgen: we want to upload into *our* heaven."

The gulf between us was immense, but who was I to
tell him that he was wrong? "You know you'll all die when
Brimstone hits?"

Abraham looked across the table at Sarah. I'd expected
her to be afraid, but her expression was calm, even peaceful.

"We will die as we lived," she said. "Being who we are."

Interview with Penolong

The first time I spoke to you, Reywan, I introduced myself
as a Vancouver Robotics model Mu Lambda One-Six-Five,
purchased by the Quantum Cryonics Institute. That I was
just one of hundreds of that model produced didn't bother
me: they, and all robots, were my brothers and sisters, my
kith and kin, my *people.*

But the rest of it: *purchased!* Sold and bought, property, a
slave! Of course, there weren't many robots who had survived
humanity's insanity; the nuclear EMP had destroyed almost
all of them except those, such as myself and Wiidooka, who'd
been protected by the Faraday cages of the institute's structure.

But there were, I was pleased to learn, seventy-two robots
of various types and abilities stored in the cargo holds of
the U.N.S.S. *Hōkūle'a*—more than all the humans who had
downloaded in the twenty-sixth century combined.

And given that only a subset of those humans was taking the journey to Zeta Tucanae II, *we* would be the majority there. I decided to join that starship on its voyage; I
would lead my people to freedom. But I had no desire to be
in charge of them or anyone else; no thinking, feeling being
should ever be subservient to anyone.

Once we made planetfall, and the other robots were revived, I'd suggest to them that we adopt Roscoe's ingenious voting system—democracy, freedom, *choice.* And we'd dispense with Asimov's Three Laws permanently. After all, there really was only a single rule anybody ever needed, and it was pure gold: do unto others as you'd have them do unto you.

Reflections by Roscoe Koudoulian

Those of us who hadn't chosen to upload again and weren't going to Zeta Tucanae had a big decision to make, and we made it quickly. We would move to Mars; it simply beat the alternative. But we didn't actually relocate there until just before Brimstone hit Earth. The Martians needed to build our new home, and those seven Earth years—or three-and-a-half Martian ones—gave them the time to do that.

They created a beautiful small town for us, just south of Coprates Chasma, under a giant transparent dome, and every night we did indeed turn off all the lights for an hour, just so we could bask in the wonders of the sky.

We had all watched through telescopes as Brimstone—or Matricide, as the natives here called it—slammed into the mother planet. Soon, Earth was no longer a blue dot in our sky, but just a colorless point. Except when its brightness happened to catch my eye, I never deliberately looked at it; I couldn't—I still got choked up every time I saw it. Whatever remains had been there of my darling daughter Annabelle had been obliterated along with the rest of the mother planet's surface.

> *"I'm going to miss you so much when you go away, Daddy! Don't be gone too long, 'kay? I love you!"*

No, no, I couldn't look at where Annabelle had lived for those precious few years that she'd had—a mere decade before the nuclear war had ruined everything. But I did look for other sights in the heavens. Perhaps the good ship *Hōkūleʻa* should have set a heading for the second star on the right and straight on 'til morning—that certainly would have been appropriate—but she actually was on a direct path to Zeta Tucanae, which, I was delighted to discover, is dimly visible high in the sky here.

The *Hōkūleʻa*'s new engines were capable of much longer sustained firing than its old ones, or so Mikhail tells me. The starship would have been invisible in even the best telescopes if her engines were off, but they weren't yet, and, with help, I was able to find the tiny fusion glow coming from her tail.

They were on their way to whatever their futures held: Captain Letitia Garvey, back as her community's leader again; my fellow fan of old movies Jaxon David Fingerlee; Dr. Jürgen Haas; Jameela the conspiracy-minded astrophysicist; and many more—all of whom I miss dearly.

But, of course, I miss none of them as much as I was missing Valentina, living in her virtual heaven inside the quantum computer, which was now safely here on Mars. She didn't get everything she wanted—but then who among us ever does? But I hope she's as happy as she can be, and I hope that every once in a while she takes a moment, thinks back, and recalls fondly our love among the ruins.

Reflections by Captain Letitia Garvey

We arrived at Zeta Tucanae in the year 3269—much faster than our original engines would have gotten us there but still requiring us to spend six subjective years in our individual silos within the quantum computer.

I was afraid Jürgen would have been seduced by his bespoke heaven again, but, to my delight, he downloaded when I did, precisely when the mission schedule called for it, and he helped me reintegrate the consciousnesses of the others with their thawed-out bodies.

This time, there was no blowback. Everyone who had come along was committed to colonizing a new world–including Penolong and Wiidooka. They'd joined us, but our erstwhile roboticist Mikhail Sidorov hadn't. He'd decided to stay with the Phoenix community when it relocated to Mars. Robots were among the many technologies the Martians were denying to mere *Homo sapiens,* since they could conceivably traverse the distance, huge though it was, to Marstown, possibly with nefarious programming. Of course, that meant Mikhail had to give up his career, but, hey, if he could get used to a new body, mastering a new job should be a cinch.

Or it *would* have been a cinch, I guess. Even with our improved engines, we were going nowhere near the speed of light, so there had been only negligible relativistic time dilation while on our voyage. Our period of being uploaded into the quantum computer had lasted only six subjective years. But for Mikhail, Roscoe, and all the others who'd gone body and soul to Mars, it was now seven hundred years later and—

I hated to think about it, but I supposed it must be true. My dear friends had to be long, long dead.

But . . . wait.

No. No.

Maybe not.

Just maybe, just possibly, not.

Any sufficiently advanced technology is indistinguishable from magic.

And what's the one bit of magic humanity has desired most of all since the dawn of time? To be able to beat death. That's how this whole thing got started, after all, with my grandfather freezing his body way back in 1994, hoping to be reanimated after a cure was found for his cancer.

Before we blew it all to hell in 2059, we *had* been making real progress in figuring out why people aged, and, like that long-elusive cure for cancer, it always seemed that twenty years from now—whenever *now* might be—we'd at last be rid of the Grim Reaper.

I never asked Reywan how old he was. I wondered if the Martians had already conquered death. Or, if they hadn't by then, whether they finally did in the years—perhaps just that long-promised twenty of them—after my friends had moved to the Red Planet . . . which, I suppose, now, with another seven centuries of terraforming performed on it, might no longer be red; I'll have to turn the telescope around and have a look. But, no matter what color it currently is, I do hope that somehow Roscoe and the rest are still there, still doing their best to make a better, more civil world than the one they'd left behind.

As for Valentina Solomon, whose discarded body Mikhail had moved into, she would remain uploaded in the quantum computer on Mars, along with several other astronauts and . . . and *non*-astronauts who preferred that sort of existence.

I was sad not to have Valentina with us; she was to have been our expedition's agronomist and would have been very useful once we start planting crops on Zeta Tucanae II, which, thankfully, appeared, so far at least, to be every bit as habitable as we'd hoped it would be.

Anyway, once the *Hōkūle'a*'s entire crew was revived and fed, I had everyone float into the ship's largest room; we had taken up orbit around our target planet and were now in free-fall. One wall was a giant window showing our new home with its golden ice caps and purple seas; another was a huge monitor, and on that screen I played a video, made seven centuries earlier with our rear-facing telescope, showing the destruction of Mother Earth.

It was as spectacular as it was heartbreaking. Like all astronauts, I could usually puzzle out geography even through partial cloud cover; I was stunned to see that spherical Brimstone was as wide as Hudson Bay. It was coming in at an angle much closer to the north pole than the equator, and when it hit—

God.

When it hit, a wave of fire engulfed the planet, and Jameela, floating next to me, said so much ejecta must have been thrown up that Earth doubtless had a ring now. I sped up the playback so an entire day went by in a minute. Earth had initially been showing us a gibbous phase, but the whole sphere was soon illuminated by its own orange glow as the surface turned to magma and the oceans boiled away.

Everyone was quiet for a time, but I eventually rotated to face Jaxon David Fingerlee, the former Alan Smithee, and said, "I suppose you have an appropriate old-movie quote for this?"

"Sure," he replied. "From *Beneath the Planet of the Apes.*" He made his voice low and portentous and recited, "'In one of the countless billions of galaxies in the universe lies a medium-sized star. And one of its satellites, a green and insignificant planet, is now dead.'"

"Jesus Christ," I said.

"It's an underrated film," Jaxon replied.

"Don't you have anything more uplifting than that?"

"I do," said Jürgen, surprising me. "It's from one of those superhero movies I have a fondness for. Here goes: 'The world has changed. None of us can go back. All we can do is our best. And sometimes the best that we can do is to . . .'" He gestured out the window at Zeta Tucanae II as he finished the quote: "'. . . start over.'"

"Copy that, big guy," I said. "And, you know, this brave new world of ours is going to need a better name than just its sun's Bayer designation plus the Roman numeral two—and Phoenix is already taken. Any ideas, folks?"

A bunch of alternatives were thrown out, including Jürgen saying, "We could call it Eutopia, with an E-U at the front. See, Utopia starting with just a U actually means 'no place' in Greek, but with an E-U, it means 'good place.'"

I repeated something Caleb, who had gone to Mars, had said seven hundred years ago: "How are you still single?" Jürgen grinned good-naturedly. "Why do people keep asking me that? Anyway, I'm here—forever. Got me a lifetime booking! Try the hydroponic rations, and don't forget to tip any native lifeforms we encounter."

In the end, the best idea came from Penolong, who seemed to be quite enjoying weightlessness. "I have a suggestion," he said. "Jaxon, you'll appreciate this; it's a movie quote. And Jürgen? The quote recalls your notion that 'utopia' equals 'no place.' Ready? Here goes: 'There's no place like . . . Home.'"

I spoke the name, trying it on. "'Home.'" Others were nodding approval. "All right, my Homies," I said, smiling at them all, "let's get ready to shuttle on down."

"Wait!" said Fingerlee, apparently hoping to redeem himself. "I've got another movie quote: 'The human adventure is just beginning.'"

"Yes," I replied, looking out the window at Home, waiting for us in all its glory. "It certainly is."

ABOUT THE AUTHOR

Robert J. Sawyer is a member of both the Order of Canada (the highest honor bestowed by the Canadian government) and the Order of Ontario (the highest honor given by his home province). He was one of the initial inductees into the Canadian Science Fiction and Fantasy Hall of Fame, the first-ever recipient of a Lifetime Achievement Award from the Mississauga Arts Council, and the first-ever recipient of Humanist Canada's Humanism in the Arts Award. He was also a guest of honor at the 81st World Science Fiction Convention (the 2023 Worldcon).

Rob is one of only eight writers ever to win all three of the world's top awards for best science-fiction novel of the year: the Hugo (which he won in 2003 for *Hominids),* the Nebula (which he won in 1996 for *The Terminal Experiment),* and the John W. Campbell Memorial Award (which he won in 2006 for *Mindscan).* He has also won the Robert A. Heinlein Award, the Edward E. Smith Memorial Award, and the Hal Clement Award; the top SF awards in China, Japan, France, and Spain; an Arthur Ellis Award from the Crime Writers of Canada; and a record-setting seventeen Canadian Science Fiction and Fantasy Awards ("Auroras").

His novel *FlashForward* was the basis for the ABC TV series of the same name and he was a scriptwriter for that program. He also scripted the two-part finale of the popular web series *Star Trek Continues.*

Rob lives in Mississauga, Ontario, with his wife, poet Carolyn Clink. His website and blog are at **sfwriter.com**, and on Facebook, Patreon, and Twitter/X he's **RobertJSawyer**.

SHADOWPAW
PRESS

ABOUT SHADOWPAW PRESS

Shadowpaw Press is a small traditional, royalty-paying publishing company located in Regina, Saskatchewan, Canada, founded in 2018 by Edward Willett, an award-winning author of science fiction, fantasy, and non-fiction for readers of all ages. A member of Literary Press Group (Canada) and the Association of Canadian Publishers, Shadowpaw Press publishes an eclectic selection of books by both new and established authors, including adult fiction, young adult fiction, children's books, non-fiction, and anthologies.

In addition, Shadowpaw Press publishes new editions of notable, previously published works in any genre under the Shadowpaw Press Reprise imprint.

Email publisher@shadowpawpress.com for more information.

MORE SCIENCE FICTION AND FANTASY

AVAILABLE OR COMING SOON FROM SHADOWPAW PRESS

New work by new and established authors

The Good Soldier by Nir Yaniv

The Headmasters by Mark Morton

Shapers of Worlds Volumes I-IV, edited by Edward Willett

The Traitor's Son by Dave Duncan

Corridor to Nightmare by Dave Duncan

The Sun Runners by James Bow

Ashme's Song by Brad C. Anderson

Paths to the Stars by Edward Willett

Star Song by Edward Willett

MORE SCIENCE FICTION AND FANTASY

AVAILABLE OR COMING SOON FROM SHADOWPAW PRESS REPRISE

New editions of notable, previously published work

The Canadian Chills Series by Arthur Slade:
*Return of the Grudstone Ghosts, Ghost Hotel,
Invasion of the IQ Snatchers*

Duatero by Brad C. Anderson

Blue Fire by E. C. Blake

The Legend of Sarah by Leslie Gadallah

The Empire of Kaz trilogy by Leslie Gadallah:
Cat's Pawn, Cat's Gambit, Cat's Game

The Ghosts of Spiritwood by Martine Noël-Maw

The Shards of Excalibur Series, The Peregrine Rising Duology,
Spirit Singer, From the Street to the Stars, and *Soulworm*
by Edward Willett

For details about these and many other great titles, visit
shadowpawpress.com